# Full Court Press

AN
ORCA
YOUNG
READER

# Full Court Press

## ERIC WALTERS

ORCA BOOK PUBLISHERS

**Canadian Cataloguing in Publication Data**
Walters, Eric, 1957–
Full court press

ISBN 1-55143-169-6

I. Title.
PS8595.A598F84 2000    jC813'.54    C00-910883-1
PZ7.W17129Fu 2000

**Library of Congress Catalog Card Number:** 00-107320

Orca Book Publishers gratefully acknowledges the support of
our publishing programs provided by the following agencies:
the Department of Canadian Heritage, The Canada Council
for the Arts, and the British Columbia Arts Council.

Cover design by Christine Toller
Cover illustration by John Mantha
Interior illustrations by Kirsti

| IN CANADA | IN THE UNITED STATES |
|---|---|
| Orca Book Publishers | Orca Book Publishers |
| PO Box 5626, Station B | PO Box 468 |
| Victoria, BC  Canada | Custer, WA   USA |
| V8R 6S4 | 98240-0468 |

02  01  00  •  5  4  3  2  1

*For my son, Nick;*
*win, lose or draw,*
*you always make me proud.*

# Chapter 1
# The Announcement

As the last strains of the national anthem faded away, we all settled into our seats to wait for the P.A. announcements.

"Good morning, Clark Boulevard students, and welcome back for another wonderful week!" said our principal, the ever-cheerful Ms. Grieve. I liked school, but it always sounded like she *really* liked it.

"I'd like to start the week by reading the names of the Clark All-Stars for the past week, those students who were caught doing something great!"

As Ms. Grieve began to list off the names I started to drift off. There were always lots and lots of students who made the list.

I looked down. Underneath my shirt I could make out the outline of my medal — my gold medal. I hadn't taken it off since it was given to me on Friday. If I had it my way I would have worn it over top of my shirt where everybody could see it, but my father said I shouldn't show it off like that. He said that winning something was like having underwear. Just 'cause you have it doesn't mean you should be waving it around over top of your head. I guess he was right … but it would have been nice just to show it off a little.

Across the room sat my best friend, Kia. She flashed me a quick smile. I knew that her medal was hanging around her neck, hidden under a heavy sweater.

"And now," Ms. Grieve continued, "Mr. Roberts has a few announcements."

I was always interested in anything our gym teacher had to say, so I snapped to attention.

"I'd like to congratulate all those who played in our three-on-three basketball tournament," he began. "Could all those who participated please stand up."

Hesitantly kids, including me and Kia, pushed back their chairs and rose to their feet. There were fifteen of us in our class, and, of course, more kids doing the same thing in other classes all around the school.

"First of all I want to say," Mr. Roberts continued, "that all those who participated in the tournament are winners. Let's give all of them a round of applause."

The kids still sitting began to clap. I heard the same sound echoing through the halls, coming from other rooms.

"That's great," Mr. Roberts said. "And I'd like everybody to now take a seat. That is everybody except for our finalists: Kingsley, Dean, Roy, Marcus, Kia and Nick."

I stopped myself halfway down and straightened up. I'd wanted to show off my medal, but now as I was standing there with all the eyes on me, I would have loved to take my seat. At least Kia was standing as well.

"We had a thrilling final game after school on Friday between two excellent teams," Mr. Roberts said. "In the end the winners were the team of Marcus, Kia and Nick. Let's give them another round of applause!"

Our classmates started to clap and cheer and even whistle. I gave a little half smile and a bit of a wave and then sunk down into my seat as the cheering faded.

"And on that note," Mr. Roberts continued, "beginning before school tomorrow we'll be having the tryouts for the school basketball team. All interested students should obtain a permission form from the office. This letter has to be signed by both your parents and your teacher. Thank you."

As the next announcement came on, I looked at Kia, and I knew what she was thinking. If only we were in grade five instead of grade three, we'd be there tomorrow. I guess we'd just have to wait until grade five.

"All right, everybody, we have plenty of work to do this morning, so let's get down to it," Mrs. Orr stated. "We'll start with spelling."

A few kids grumbled, while some of the others were slow to get out their books.

"Please don't worry about not getting your work done," Mrs. Orr said loudly. "There is plenty of time to finish your work ... during recess, at lunch, and then after school."

I knew she wasn't joking around. In this class you had two choices: finish your work, or lose your free time finishing your work. I pulled out my spelling and started.

★ ★ ★

The recess bell rang out just as I finished my last math question and put down my pencil. I got up and hurried to Mrs. Orr's desk, joining the line of kids waiting to have their work checked so they could go out for recess. Kia was right behind me.

"Soccer or basketball?" she whispered.

"How about foot hockey?" I suggested, turning around to talk to her.

"I guess ... if we can play soccer at lunch recess or —"

"Nick, are you hoping to go out for recess?"

I turned back around. I was next in line. Quickly I stepped forward and handed Mrs. Orr my books — spelling and math — the work for the first quarter of the day.

She ran her finger along the column of answers.

"All done, Nicholas. You're free."

I walked over to get my coat. I was in no rush since I wasn't going to go out until she'd checked Kia's work too.

"Oh, and Nicholas ...," Mrs. Orr said.

I turned back around.

"I just wanted you to know — both you

and Kia — that you have my permission to try out for the basketball team."

"We do?" Kia questioned.

"Of course. You both have satisfactory marks and a good attitude toward school. I just expect that you'll not let these practices get in the way of your schoolwork."

Kia and I exchanged a confused look.

"But Mrs. Orr," I said. "We're in grade three."

"I'm aware of your grade."

"Yeah, of course," I stammered. "I just mean that the school team is for grade fives."

"It is?" Mrs. Orr asked.

"It was last year," Kia said.

"I just thought it would be for the best players in the school," Mrs. Orr said.

Kia looked at me. "Do you think that we could?"

I shrugged. "I don't know. Maybe."

"Then maybe we should be playing basketball at recess," Kia suggested.

"I'm afraid not," Mrs. Orr said, shaking her head. "You missed questions four through eight, so you'll be spending your recess in here finishing up your math," she said as she handed Kia back her book.

# Chapter 2
# To Try or Not to Try

"I'm not sure what the big decision is about," my mother said as she started to clear away the supper dishes.

"I just assumed that you two would try out for any basketball team, anywhere, anytime," she continued.

"It's not that simple," I said as I started to put plates into the dishwasher.

"It's the *school* team," Kia added.

"And that's a fortunate coincidence, since you both go to the school," Mom said. "So what's the problem?"

"You don't understand. The team is for the grade fives. It's sort of a senior team," I explained.

"It's a rule? You two aren't allowed to try out for the team?" Mom asked.

"No ... I don't think it's a rule or anything. It's more like ... like a tradition."

"A tradition?" she questioned. "Thanksgiving dinner with your in-laws, or sending out Christmas cards, or wedding showers are traditions. I think that a school team should have the best players in the school, even if they are in kindergarten."

"Come on, Mom, kindergarten kids couldn't make the team."

"But maybe a couple of grade three students could. You two are among the best players in the whole school, aren't you?" Mom asked.

"Not the best," I answered.

"But you two were on the best three-on-three team in the school. Along with Marcus you won the tournament, so doesn't that make you two of the best three players?" she asked.

"Well ... like you said, Marcus was on our team," I explained.

"And he is the *best* player in the whole school," Kia added. "Without him we never would have had a chance of winning."

"I see," my mother said. "So there's no question that Marcus will make the school team."

"Oh, for sure," I agreed, and Kia nodded her head in agreement.

"And I assume that some of the other students in the school are pretty good too," my mother continued.

"A few," Kia said.

"Yeah. Kingsley is really good, and there's Dean, and probably Adam Thompson, and —"

"And Kyle is pretty good, too," Kia said.

"Yeah, Kyle too," I agreed.

"So that makes five," my mother said. "And how many players will be on the team?"

"I don't know. At least ten, maybe twelve," I answered.

"So that means there are still somewhere between five and seven spots open. Are there that many other kids in the school who are better than you two?"

"No way!" Kia said.

I shook my head. "Not that many."

"You don't sound as confident as Kia," my mother said.

I never sounded as confident as Kia did

because I never *felt* as confident as she did. She was always that way — completely sure of success until she failed. Me, I was sort of the opposite. Completely positive it wasn't going to work, until the final moment of surprising success. I knew that Kia was already convinced we should try out for the team, and that I was probably fighting a losing battle at this point. I just didn't know. This wasn't just the big kids at our school, but the big kids at *other* schools.

"So you two not wanting to try out for the team has nothing to do with being afraid of not making the team?" Mom questioned.

"Of course not!" Kia exclaimed.

"No, that isn't it," I agreed.

"Then what is it?" Mom asked.

"It's just … just that if we make the team we'll be playing against other schools," I said.

"That is the idea behind a school team," she said.

"It's just that we saw a couple of those other teams when they played against our school last year," I explained.

"And?"

"It's just … just that they were … big."

"Really big," Kia agreed.

I was glad that she at least agreed with that.

"Bigger than the kids in your school?"

I tried to picture anybody being bigger than Kingsley, or Roy, who were about the biggest kids in our school.

"I think they were bigger," Kia said.

"Or maybe they just *seemed* bigger because you two were smaller. You were only in grade two last year when you were watching those games. Now you're bigger ... grade three bigger."

"Well, we are bigger than last year," I admitted. "Although a lot smaller than the grade fives in our school, and probably every other school too."

"But size doesn't mean everything," my mother said.

"Mom, this is basketball, not chess. If I was seven feet tall, this wouldn't be a problem."

"Well, being smaller than the kids at our school didn't stop us from winning the three-on-three tournament," Kia added, agreeing with my mother.

Great, now there were two of them arguing on the other side.

"So are you two going to try out for the

team or not?" Mom asked.

I looked at Kia. Of course, I already knew what she was thinking.

"It looks like we're going to try," I said.

My mother flashed us a smile and then started to laugh.

"What's so funny?" I asked.

"I just thought that this is the strangest conversation I think we've ever had. With all the basketball you play, at school, on the driveway and on the rep team, here I am trying to convince the two of you that you need to try to play *more* basketball."

"That is a bit strange," I admitted. She was always telling me that I played too much b-ball.

"Maybe I should hope that you two don't make the team," she said.

"Mom!"

"I'm just kidding. Beside, there are lots of worse things in life than not making a team."

I nodded my head in agreement. I knew of one thing that was worse. Making the team and getting killed by one of the other teams, and I didn't mean just on the scoreboard.

# Chapter 3
# The Try-Outs

Kia's father dropped us off at the curb in front of the school. Kia waved as he drove off. I looked at my watch. It was ten minutes to eight. I had never been to the school this early and it seemed strange. There were only a couple of cars in the normally full parking lot. I recognized one. It belonged to our principal, Ms. Grieve. I wasn't surprised it was there. I think she practically lived at the school.

And of course it wasn't just the parking lot that was empty. There was nobody in the playground, or on the street walking toward the school.

"Tryouts did start this morning ... right?" I asked.

"Of course, they're on today ... I'm pretty sure."

We walked up to the front doors. I tried to pull one open. It wouldn't budge. It was locked. Kia grabbed the other door. She repeatedly pulled at it, and the door bumped and rocked slightly, but it wouldn't open. It was locked as well.

"What time does the school normally open?" Kia asked.

"I don't know. I just know it's always open by the time I get here. What are we going to do?"

"Maybe we should try another door," Kia suggested. "How about the one closest to the gym?"

That made sense. Besides we certainly had time to kill. We cut across the grass and passed by our principal's office. I glanced through the window. I could see her sitting at her desk, working. Just as we got to the corner of the building I thought I heard voices. We hurried around, arriving just in time to see the door by the gym close.

"Come on," I said as we sprinted for the

door.

Kia got there a split second before me and pulled the door open. Instantly we could hear the sounds of people talking and balls bouncing. We followed the noise down the hall and into the gym. The place was filled with kids!

"It looks like every kid in grade five is here," I said quietly to Kia.

"But nobody from grade three, or even grade four," she answered. "There must be twenty kids here."

"Nineteen including you and me."

"You counted?"

"It's one of my skills," I said.

The door opened behind us and three more kids — grade five kids — entered the gym.

"Twenty, twenty-one and twenty-two," Kia said. "I've mastered that counting stuff too. And have you noticed how many of them are girls?"

"Girls?"

"As in not boys," Kia said sarcastically.

"Well, none … except for you, of course. Were you expecting one of the other girls to be here?"

"It would have been nice," she said.

"Who did you think would try out?"

She didn't answer right away and then shrugged. "I guess I didn't really expect anybody. It's just that it's strange to always be the only girl all the time."

"It would be a little different," I agreed.

"A little different? What would it be like if you were the only guy in the gym and everybody else was a girl?"

"Now that would be strange," I admitted. "But wouldn't that be even stranger for you?"

Kia chuckled to herself. "Probably. Let's get ready."

We walked to the front of the gym, moving around kids and watching as we walked. Nobody seemed to even notice us. We climbed up onto the edge of the stage, took a seat and started to put on our basketball shoes.

"Can you believe some of the people who are trying out?" Kia asked.

"There are some surprises," I admitted. We'd played against most of these kids in the three-on-three contest, or at least seen them play. Some of them were not what I'd call 'quality' players.

16

"There's Marcus," Kia said, pointing to the far corner.

He was bouncing a ball, standing and talking to a group of kids that included Kingsley and Dean and Roy. Great, Roy trying out too. Though I didn't really know him — 'cause he was in grade five — Roy was not my favorite guy. He had been part of the team that we'd beaten in the finals and had been pretty dirty and nasty — and not just in our games.

"I see your old buddy is here," Kia said, reading my mind.

"Roy doesn't like you any better than he likes me."

"I don't think Roy likes even his own mother," Kia said, "but it wasn't me who made him look like a fool in front of half the school during the final game of the tournament."

"I didn't make him look … at least I didn't *mean* to make him look bad," I said.

"What you meant and what you did are two different things, but I'm sure Roy will be just as forgiving as he is nice."

"But he's not nice at …" I let the sentence trail off, because of course Kia was saying that he probably would hold a grudge.

"And maybe we can all become teammates and good friends," she continued. "And then you can invite Roy to come back to your house after the games for milk and —"

A shrill whistle blast interrupted Kia's comments. It was Mr. Roberts, standing at the gym door, a ball under one arm, a whistle in his other hand. Most kids had stopped talking and turned to face him. A couple were still bouncing their balls.

"Hold the balls!" Mr. Roberts bellowed and the bouncing stopped. "Everybody line up right across the baseline!"

Kia and I jumped down off the edge of the stage and took a place at the very end.

"Welcome to the first basketball tryout," Mr. Roberts said as he started to walk down the line. "It's great that so many of you want to be on the team. Unfortunately you all cannot be part of the team. There are only ten spots available."

Ten spots meant two less possibilities for me and Kia. This had suddenly gotten harder before it had even started.

"We will be meeting before and after school all week. After Friday's last workout I'll be making my decisions about who will be on the team. A list will be posted on the gym door Monday morning. I know that some people will not be —"

Mr. Roberts stopped mid-sentence as he came to the end of the line and saw me and Kia. He looked confused.

"Nick ... Kia ... I didn't expect to see the two of you here this morning."

"Where else would we be?" Kia asked.

"It's just that you're in grade three."

"But we're allowed to tryout, aren't we?" I asked.

"Well, sure ... I guess ... anybody in the school can try out."

"Good," Kia said. "Because we want to be on the team."

Mr. Roberts nodded his head in agreement, but there was something about the look on his face that said he had some serious doubts.

"Okay, we've wasted enough time. We're going to do some warm-ups and then once everybody is good and loose we're going to do some suicides. Let's get going!"

★★★

I took a deep swig from my bottle of water. It felt good going down. Mr. Roberts hadn't even let us stop for a water break during the whole tryout.

"That was some workout," Kia commented.

I nodded my head and then took a towel out of my bag to wipe the sweat off my face.

"Mr. Roberts was pretty tough," Kia said.

"Yeah, he was." I didn't say anything, but I thought he was especially tough on the two of us.

"All right, everybody!" Mr. Roberts. "Get to class. The bell be going shortly."

Kids started to move more quickly, gathering up their things and heading for the door.

A couple of times during the workout I'd heard comments from kids about us being there. I think it was even worse for Kia. Some of the guys had made snide remarks about Kia being a girl. Maybe it was bad enough to be competing with a grade three, but a grade three *girl* seemed to make it even worse. I hadn't really thought about it much before — I hardly even thought of Kia as a girl — but it must have been even harder for her to try out for the team.

Kia and I started out along with the few remaining stragglers.

"Nick, Kia," Mr. Roberts called out. "Could I speak to you to for a minute."

The last few kids exited the gym, leaving us alone with Mr. Roberts. I wasn't sure what he wanted to say, but I was pretty sure I wouldn't like it. Had he decided to cut us already?

"I just wanted to talk to the two of you for a few minutes," he began. "I'm a little concerned about the two of you being on the team. You know we'll be playing against other schools, right?"

"Yeah, of course," Kia said.

"And I'm just worried about the fact that the other school teams will all be made up of older and bigger kids."

"We know," I said.

"I don't want you two getting hurt. Those kids won't know the two of you and they won't necessarily be as gentle with you as the kids at our school were during the three-on-three tournament."

"Gentle?" I asked. I still had sore ribs on one side from where Roy had elbowed me in the last game of the three-on-three tournament.

"These games will be very serious."

"No more serious than the games our rep team plays," Kia said.

"But the difference is that you play those games against kids your own age, right?" Mr. Roberts asked.

"Yeah. We play in a league where every-body is the same age. The older kids play minor-bantam."

"That's what I thought," Mr. Roberts said. "I just don't know if I want to take respon-sibility if one of you gets hurt."

"But we have letters of permission from our parents," I said, pulling the form out of my pocket.

"This piece of paper will protect me, but it won't protect you," Mr. Roberts said. "The other schools are going to take advantage of your size, or I guess your lack of size. They're going to put somebody big on you to shove you around, intimidate you, create a mismatch ... at least that's what I'd do."

Of course he was right. That's what any good coach would do.

"Is there any way I can talk you two out of this?" Mr. Roberts asked.

"Nope," Kia said decisively.

I nodded my head in agreement, although he had almost convinced me. I liked basketball. I didn't like getting smacked around.

"In that case you're welcome to come to the rest of the tryouts."

"Thanks," I said.

"Just keep in mind that coming out isn't a guarantee of making the team. Winning the three-on-three tournament last week means absolutely nothing. You're going to have to earn your spot on the team."

"We understand," Kia said.

"And just because you're younger doesn't mean I'm going to take it easier on you. If anything I'm going to be harder."

I nodded my head. I thought that was what he'd already done in the first practice.

"And even if you do make the team, you can't expect to get much playing time. You'll be well down the bench. Do you understand all that?"

"We understand," I said and Kia mumbled agreement.

"And you still want to come to the tryouts?" Mr. Roberts asked.

"We do," Kia said.

"Then I'll see you two right after school.

Don't be late or you'll have to run laps. And speaking of late, you both better get going or you're going to be late for —"

His words were cut off by the loud ringing of the bell.

"Tell Mrs. Orr that you were late because you were talking to me," Mr. Roberts said.

"We're not late yet," I said. "We just have to get to class before the national anthem starts."

"See you later, sir," Kia said as we rushed out of the gym.

We hurried along the hall toward our room.

"That wasn't very encouraging," Kia said as we walked.

"That's an understatement. He basically said that he didn't want us on the team, and he'd be really tough on us during the tryouts, and even if we do make the team, either the other team will be shoving us around, or we'll be spending most of our time on the bench." I paused. "Do you still think we should try?"

"What do you think?"

"I think we should —"

Suddenly I was grabbed from the back, spun around and slammed against the wall.

# Chapter 4
# Welcome to my World

"Leave him alone!" Kia yelled.

"Shut up!" Roy snapped at her, but he did let go of me. "I wanted to have a little conversation with you two."

"Maybe we don't want to talk to you," Kia said.

"That's no problem, because I'm going to do all the talking and you two are going to do all the listening."

"We don't have time for either," I said. "If we don't hurry, we'll be late for class."

"Stay where you are or you're going to be late in a whole different way. Like in dead, departed, the late," Roy said.

"Please stand for the national anthem," the P.A. crackled.

Now it was official. We were late. I looked up and down the hall. There was nobody else in sight.

"I don't like you two," Roy said, wagging a finger in my face.

Now *there* was news.

"And I'm liking you even less by the minute. What's the big idea about coming out this morning?"

"We were just trying out for the team," I said.

"That team is only for grade fives," Roy snapped.

"Mr. Roberts said we were welcome to try out," Kia said.

"I don't care what Mr. Roberts said. I'm telling you that I don't want you two on my team!"

"Your team?" Kia questioned. "What makes you think you'll even make the team?"

I had to hand it to Kia. She had more guts than me. Then again, it would be my guts on the floor if Roy was mad.

"You better hope I make the team," Roy said ominously. "Because if you two make

the team and I don't … believe me, I won't be happy. Understand?" he asked as he poked me hard in the chest with a finger.

"I … I understand," I stammered. There wasn't a lot of room to not understand. "Maybe we could all be on the team together."

"Forget it! I don't want to be on the same team with you!"

"You can't threaten us," Kia said.

"It looks like I just did. Besides," Roy said with a smirk, "this isn't a threat … it's a promise."

He stepped forward until he stood right over top of me. I stumbled back a few inches into the wall. At that instant the national anthem ended and I was now free to run — or at least try to run.

"I'm going to —"

"Why aren't you three in class?"

Roy stepped back and we all turned around to see Mr. White, our music teacher, walking toward us. I was so grateful to see him.

"Why are you just standing there?" Mr. White asked.

"We were just coming from basketball practice," Kia said.

"And Mr. Roberts wanted to talk to us

after the practice, so we were a little later than everybody else," I explained.

"And then we had to stop and wait in the hall until the national anthem was finished," Roy added. "You didn't want us to walk when that was playing, did you?"

His voice was taunting. Not exactly the right tone to take with a teacher.

"No, of course not. But you're supposed to be in class before it starts, so you were already late. Now get to class!"

"See you at recess," Roy said under as his breath as he turned and walked away.

"But first," Mr. White called out, and we stopped and turned around. "Go to the office to get late slips."

"The office!" Roy snapped. "Come on, give me a break!"

"Sure thing," Mr. White said. "Your break starts right now. Kia and Nick go to the office. Roy, you and I are going to have a little chat ... *before* you go to the office."

I started to smirk, but Roy's glare wiped it off my face.

★★★

As quietly as two little mice, we walked in

30

through the rear door of the classroom. Mrs. Orr just barely threw a glance our way as she continued to explain to the class the work for the morning. Kia and I joined the rest of the class on the carpet.

"We're going to change our routine this morning," Mrs. Orr said. "I want everybody to start the day off with silent reading."

We hardly had time to put our bottoms down on the floor. I got up with everybody else and headed to my desk and —

"Nicholas and Kia, please stay behind," Mrs. Orr said. "I need to talk to the two of you."

There wasn't much question what this was about. Mrs. Orr hated late. Late assignments, late projects, and especially late people.

"Were you two at the basketball tryout this morning?" Mrs. Orr asked.

"Yes," I said.

"And am I to expect that the two of you will be late for the rest of the week?"

"Just today! Mr. Roberts wanted to talk to us after the tryout and —"

"We'll be on time every day for sure!" I said, cutting Kia off.

"Good. Because if you're going to be late and disrupt the class every morning I'd have to withdraw the permission I gave for you to try out for the team."

"Please don't do that!" Kia pleaded.

"I've given my permission and it will stand … for now. But I expect you to follow the usual routines and expectations of the class. You must be on time every morning. Am I understood?"

"Completely," Kia said, as I nodded in agreement.

Maybe it would have been better if she'd said we couldn't go out for the team. Then I wouldn't have to worry about not making the team — or worry about making it. Either option didn't look too good.

"You'll certainly have time to make up for the two minutes you missed this morning," Mrs. Orr said. "Because you both will stay in for first recess."

Kia opened her mouth to say something but didn't. Personally I was just happy to be inside. At least as long as I knew Roy was outside.

★★★

The room faded to silence as the last kid

exited and headed out for recess. Kia was at her desk, at the far side of the class, reading, while I put the finishing touches on my spelling. I figured since I wasn't going out anyway there was no point in busting my hump to complete everything. Besides, my head had been preoccupied. I'd been thinking about the tryout, and what Mr. Roberts had said, and of course our conversation with Roy.

"I have to do some photocopying," Mrs. Orr said as she rose from her desk. "I expect you to remain silent and working."

We listened as the sounds of her shoes clicked down the hall, getting quieter with each step, until I couldn't hear them at all.

"I was thinking," Kia said softly.

"That's good, because it is a school and they like you to do that here."

"Funny. I mean about basketball. I was wondering if we can make the team."

"Me too," I admitted.

"And not because we're not good enough, but because nobody seems to want us there."

"Maybe Marcus does," I said.

"Maybe," she said, "but it's pretty clear that even Mr. Roberts isn't on our side, any more than any of the other grade fives."

"You can't judge the whole grade by Roy."

"I'm not. At least Roy was honest about it."

"What do you mean honest?" I asked.

"He doesn't want us on the team and he told us. The rest just didn't say anything."

"I'm still not following you."

"Didn't you notice how nobody even spoke to us during the practice?"

"Not really," I said, shaking my head, but come to think of it, she was right. "I guess I was just concentrating on the drills."

"Well I noticed. You've got to remember that it wasn't just Roy we beat in the three-on-three contest. It was every single kid who was there in the gym this morning. Either their team lost to us or to another team that then lost to us."

"I hadn't thought of that," I said.

"Maybe it's time you did."

"I'm more worried about Roy. Do you think we should tell somebody?" I asked.

"We can't do that," Kia said. "First off, do you want to be known as a snitch?"

"Of course not!"

"And second, what did he really say?"

"Well ... that he didn't want us to try out

for the team."

"Yeah," Kia asked. "So what?"

"But he threatened me."

"And what exactly did he say?" Kia asked.

"He said he'd see me at recess."

"Big deal. I'm *seeing* you right now, that doesn't mean I'm going to hurt you, does it?"

"I guess not," I admitted reluctantly.

"Roy's being smart," Kia said.

"Roy and smart are two words I don't think of as going together."

"But he is. He's saying things in a way that you know what he means, but you can't prove it. I don't think he'll do anything more than talk, at least until the team is picked."

"So after that he might do something."

"He might," Kia said. "It all depends on who makes the team and who doesn't. Until then there's nothing more we can do."

"I guess you're right."

"Well, unless if I'm wrong and he *does* beat you up, then we can do something."

# Chapter 5
# From Bad to Worse

I ran back up the gym floor and took a spot at the end of the line. Other people waiting their turn were talking, or even quietly joking around. Nobody joked around with me. Nobody was friendly to me. I knew everybody, and everybody knew me, but nobody seemed to want to do anything more than grunt at me.

"That's it!" Mr. Roberts yelled out. "Let's call it a night!"

I walked over and took a seat beside Kia on the edge of the stage. She looked as tired as I felt. And if I thought Mr. Roberts had been tougher on Kia and me in the morning, I knew it for sure now. It seemed like he didn't think we could do anything right. 'Run faster, Nick,' 'Dig deeper, Kia,' 'Come on, Nick, put the pass on the mark,' 'Kia, you should have had that shot.'

Trying out for the team was never a great idea, but it had fallen way down the scale to really, really bad. Maybe we should just quit and make everybody happy.

"Let's get going," Kia said.

She didn't even sound like her usual self. She sounded sort of … I don't know … down or defeated.

"You coming over to my place for a snack?" I asked.

"Yeah, but I can only stay for a while. I'm really tired and I think I want to get to bed early."

"After finishing your homework," I said.

"Of course. Our usual work and then the extra assignment."

Besides our regular work — reading, journal and ten math problems — Kia and I had an additional assignment. Mrs. Orr had come back and caught us talking at recess and we had to write about why that was wrong.

We left the gym and started to circle around

the school to head home. I didn't feel like talking and it seemed like Kia felt the same. That was unusual and more than a little bit —

"Hi, guys!"

I spun around, jumping up into the air and — it was Marcus! Thank goodness.

"You always this jumpy?" Marcus asked.

"Not always." I'd thought Roy might be waiting for us and Marcus popping out like that had startled me.

"You two did well today," Marcus said.

"We did?" I asked.

"Yeah, better than most," he added.

"I don't think Mr. Roberts would agree with you," Kia said.

"Just because he yelled at you a couple of times?" Marcus asked.

"More than a couple."

"It's nothing to worry about. I just wanted to tell you that I think it's great you're trying out for the team. I just wish I'd tried to do it myself last year when I was in grade four."

I hadn't even thought about the fact that Marcus hadn't been on the team last year.

"I'd heard that it was only for grade fives, so I didn't even try. I know I had the skill to make that team last year. I guess I just didn't have the guts like you two."

"Guts? Us?" I asked in amazement. The only thing I knew about my guts was that they kept on rumbling whenever I thought about this whole thing.

"Not everybody is happy about us trying out for the team," Kia said.

"You're wrong there," Marcus said.

"I am?"

"Yeah. Except for me, I don't think *anybody* wants you on the team."

"I told you," Kia said to me smugly.

I turned to Marcus. "At least you're on our side."

Marcus looked down at the ground. "That was actually what I wanted to talk about ... out here ... without anybody else around." He paused. "I really would like you two to make the team. I'm on your side, but my friends aren't."

"I thought we were your friends," Kia said.

"You are! For sure!" Marcus said. "It's just that I'm still getting some heat from my friends — my grade five friends — about teaming up with you two for the tournament."

I didn't say anything, but I thought I understood.

"So I wanted you to know I might not be cheering for you out loud, but I am cheering for you inside. I better get going. "

Marcus walked off across the schoolyard. This was getting worse, and worse, and worse and …

★★★

"How's it going?"

I turned around to see my father standing at my bedroom door.

"Okay. Slow, but okay," I replied.

He walked in and sat down on the chair beside my desk where I was finishing up my homework.

"It seems like you have more homework all the time."

"Not all the time. Some days more than others," I said. What I didn't mention was the extra assignment for being late and then talking today.

"So did you have fun today?" he asked.

"About the same as usual … oh, you meant with basketball."

He nodded his head.

"I don't know if fun is the right word. The tryouts were hard, really hard."

"That's good."

"It is?"

"Of course. Hard workouts will separate those who can play from those who can't play, so you and Kia should stand out."

"Well ... we did get Mr. Roberts' attention today," I said, without saying how we had gotten his attention.

"So you figure you have a good shot at making the team."

"I didn't say that. No grade threes, or even grade fours, have ever made the team before. There's some really, really good players in grade five."

My father's face became thoughtful, and he slowly nodded his head.

"Making the team isn't that important," he said.

"What?" I'd heard the words, just couldn't believe them coming out of my father's mouth.

"Making the team isn't —"

"I heard. I just don't understand," I said, interrupting him.

"It would be nice if you made the team,

but that isn't the important part."

"Than what is?"

"Trying. Being there, putting yourself on the line and attempting something that's difficult. Are you and Kia trying your hardest?"

"Of course!"

"Then that's what matters. You give it your best shot and if you're not named to the team, then at least you walk away with your head held high."

"I guess that makes sense," I admitted.

"Good. How about you finish up some work while I go downstairs and make us two humungous bowls of chocolate ice cream?"

"With a little whipped cream on top?"

"Nope." He smiled. "A *lot* of whipped cream. How long till you're finished?"

"No more than five minutes."

"That'll just give me enough time to get them ready. Hurry up," he said as he got up.

I turned back to my work. What he'd said should have been encouraging, but it wasn't. I'd been thinking that the best thing that could happen with the tryouts was to either quit now, or just sort of go through the motions so I wouldn't make the team. Now those were no longer choices.

# Chapter 6
# Maybe ... Maybe Not

Mr. Roberts blew his whistle. The shrieking blasted off the walls and echoed around until everybody had stopped.

"It isn't that tricky!" Mr. Roberts yelled. "Let me explain it one more time."

We'd been divided into three columns and were supposed to execute a drill called the weave. So far it hadn't been working very well. Mr. Roberts walked to the front of the middle group.

"It's very simple. The man in the middle starts with the ball. He then passes it to one of the other two men — players. And all you do is follow the pass, taking the spot occupied by the player who just received the pass, while that player moves into the center spot. And this pattern continues as you move down the court until the final man lays up the ball. Any questions?"

Nobody said a word, but, judging from the expressions on kids' faces, there wasn't much doubt that there was still a lot of doubt.

"Okay, let's try it again," Mr. Roberts said. He tossed a ball to the man in the middle and then stepped out of the way.

Dean took the ball, bounced it a few times, tossed it to the player on his left, and then instantly turned and started to run to the right and — the whistle blasted and everybody stopped again.

"Can't anybody do this right?" Mr. Roberts demanded. "Anybody?"

Everybody looked down to the ground except Kia. She stuck up her hand and motioned for me to do the same. Reluctantly I put up my hand. Marcus did the same.

"Good. Let's see it work."

Marcus took up a spot in the middle while Kia and I moved separately to spots off to opposite sides. Marcus took a ball off the kid who was supposed to start the next rush.

"Now," Mr. Roberts said.

Marcus fired a pass to Kia, and then crossed over behind her as she moved into the center lane. Kia caught it chest height, bounced the ball once and then lined a pass to me. I grabbed it, took a step and fired it to Marcus who'd shifted back into the center. He put the ball to Kia who took two steps and laid it off the backboard and into the net.

"Perfect!" Mr. Roberts yelled. "That's how you do a weave!"

Kia gave me a high five as we started back up the side of the gym to take our places at the end of the lines.

"Now if we can just have some more of the grade fives do this drill right," Mr. Roberts continued. "Maybe I should just go out and get some more grade threes to try out for the team!"

I looked over at Kia. I could tell she was thinking exactly what I was thinking: if they didn't like us before, this certainly wasn't going to help.

"If we ever get this drill right," Mr. Roberts yelled, "we'll finish today with a scrimmage!"

★★★

I broke behind a screen and headed for the hoop. I was completely open. I raised my hands high to let the ball carrier know I was open and prepared for the pass and — the ball went in the completely opposite direction. Again.

A shot went up, clanked loudly off the backboard and bounced away, the rebound eaten up by a member of the other team. I hustled back on defense. Running back I briefly locked my eyes with Kia, sitting on the other team's bench. She'd had about as many touches of the ball as I'd had.

My man, Scott, brought the ball up court. I met him just past the center line, trying to angle him toward the side line. He faked for the center, and cut for the side, but didn't change hands. I reached out, poked the ball away and lunged for it. I grabbed the ball as Scott and I scrambled for it.

Out of the corner of my eye I saw a player wearing a blue bib — somebody on my side — and heaved the ball to him, just as I was bowled over as Scott and I collided. I flew through the air, landing heavily on my side and sliding along the floor. I looked up in time to see a player laying the ball into the hoop.

I struggled to my feet. My left leg hurt, and I looked down to see a nasty floor burn extending the whole way from just below the line of my shorts to my knee. Maybe I better sit down or —

A shrill blast of the whistle brought the game to a stop.

"That's it for this afternoon!" Mr. Roberts called out. "Good practice, everybody!"

I limped toward the stage to retrieve my stuff.

"Nice pass," Mr. Roberts said as I walked by him.

"Thanks," I mumbled back.

"That leg doesn't look very good."

"It's nothing," I said. I was working at not letting my face show how much it really did hurt.

"Maybe I better get the first-aid kit," Mr. Roberts suggested.

I shook my head. "It's no big deal. See you tomorrow."

KIRSTÉ

# Chapter 7
# Oh Yeah!

"Well, it's all done," Kia said.

We'd been to every tryout all week long.

"Now the hard part," I said. "The waiting."

The list would be posted on the gym door on Monday morning. I guess I should have been grateful for the weekend. Not only would I have a break from school and basketball, but I'd have a chance for my wounds to heal.

My tongue went to the spot in my mouth where it had been all cut up yesterday. I'd caught an elbow in the face — Roy's elbow — when I was going up for a rebound. I can still picture that expression on his face as I looked up at him from the floor — that satisfied smirk.

Of course, that was just one of the injuries I'd picked up. My leg was still smarting from the burn, and my side was sore from when I'd been shoved off the court and hit the bleachers.

It wasn't that anybody except Roy was trying to hurt me. It was just that everybody was bigger, and when a big body and a little body came together, the little body was most often the one that got hurt. Maybe Mr. Roberts had been right about us not being on the team. I couldn't expect anybody from other schools to be any nicer.

"So do you think we did enough?" Kia asked.

"We did all we could. You did well today."

"Yeah, I did," Kia agreed.

She'd made her shots from the outside and pulled down some rebounds.

"How do you think I did today?" I asked.

"You were … okay."

"Okay? Was it *okay* the way I stole the ball from you during the scrimmage?"

Kia didn't answer.

I had taken away a couple of balls, as

well as scored six points, pulled down four boards, and assisted on three other baskets. I think that qualified as much better than just *okay*.

"I was wondering what it would be like if only one of us made the team," Kia said.

"I hadn't even thought about that. I just figured it would be both of us or neither of us," I admitted.

"I've thought about it since the morning when my mother mentioned it to *me* over breakfast. I think most of the spots are already taken."

"Mr. Roberts said that?" I asked.

"No, I've just been trying to figure it out myself."

"We don't need many spots. Just two," I said.

"I just don't know if there are still two spots left," Kia said. "I've been making a mental list."

"And who's on your list?"

"There are the obvious ones."

"Like Marcus, Kingsly, Dean, Bojan and Mohammed," I suggested.

"Those five are a lock," she agreed.

"Probably the five starters. Who else is

on your list?"

"Scott and Kyle."

"Maybe … probably," I agreed.

"And Rajinder and Roy would have a —"

"Roy!" I exclaimed.

"Yeah, Roy. If you haven't noticed, he's not that bad a player."

"He's a jerk!" I snapped.

"I'm not arguing that, but we're talking about his basketball skills. He's good under the hoop, can rebound, is rough and has an attitude."

"Of course he has an attitude — a bad attitude," I said.

"That depends. He doesn't like losing and if he's on your side you might think that's a good attitude to have. And if I'm right, then that only leaves one spot on the roster," Kia said.

"I don't like that. I just thought it would be the two of us together, like always."

"Me too."

We walked along in silence as the thought of us being separately sunk in. What would it like to be on the team without Kia? Who would I talk to? Who would I walk home with after practice?

"I hate walking home from school without you," Kia said, practically reading my mind.

"I can't even remember the last time we didn't come home together."

"I can. Last May. You were sick."

"But we won't be able to any time there's a practice or game," I said. "And Mr. Roberts said they'd be one or the other almost every night for the whole season."

"I'd still come over to your place. It would just be later after the practices, and because I'll be later then I'll be hungrier."

"You might even want to drop into your place for a snack before you come to my place," I suggested.

"Why would I do that? It would take me even longer to practice, go home and then go to your place."

"So you think you'll be the one who makes the team and I won't?" I asked in shock.

"I could be wrong," Kia said with a shrug. "Maybe I won't make the team either."

"Or maybe I'll be the only one who's selected."

"I guess that could happen," she said.

"You guess? Since when did you think you were better than me?"

"I didn't say I was better than you."

"Good because —"

"I just think I'm a better choice for what the team needs," Kia said, cutting me off.

"What do you mean by that?" I demanded.

"You're good under the basket, getting rebounds and driving the hoop," she said.

"Yeah …"

"And I've got a better outside shot than you."

I couldn't really argue with that. She did have a good jump shot.

"So what's your point?" I asked.

"They already have a bunch of guys who are bigger than you who can get rebounds. But me, I'm one of the few people out there who can hit from the outside."

"I do more than go under the net. I can shoot too, and pass and cover and —"

"And so can I," Kia said, cutting me off again.

I hated when she did that.

"I just know which one of us won the last game of one-on-one we played," I said.

"That was months ago," Kia objected.

It was almost three months ago. We stopped playing against each other because neither one of us was a good loser — or a good winner either.

"I also know who won the second last game we played," Kia said.

"And I know which one of us has won more of the games than the other," I snapped.

"You do?" she asked.

"Yes, I do, and you're looking at him! I've won twenty-eight of the thirty-nine games we're played over the last two years."

"You've been keeping track of who's won and lost?" Kia asked in amazement.

I suddenly felt very embarrassed.

"At least if you were counting, you should have counted right," she said. "It's only twenty-five to fourteen."

"No," I said shaking my head. "I've won twenty-eight games to … wait a second … how do you know how many games you won?"

"I couldn't count on you to keep it straight, anymore than I can count on you to sink your shots from the outside," she said.

"Really! Then maybe there's something else you shouldn't count on."

"What's that?" Kia questioned.

"Coming over to my place for a snack," I said as I stomped off by myself.

# Chapter 8
# The Team

Last summer when we went to Nova Scotia for two weeks — that had been the last time I'd gone more than a day without talking to Kia.

She hadn't come over after school on Friday, or called or come over on either Saturday or Sunday. I knew how stubborn she could be. My mother always said that Kia was one of the two most stubborn people she'd ever known. She considered me the other one. Of course, that meant that we'd had our fights over the years. After all, we'd been friends for five years, but those fights had never lasted this long.

My mom had figured out something was wrong within two seconds of me walking in the door after school on Friday. She'd yelled out, 'Hi, Nick ... hi, Kia!' from the other room, and when only one of us answered back, it didn't take Sherlock Holmes to know something was different. She asked me what had happened and I told her I didn't want to talk about it. Of course, not wanting to talk about it, and having to talk about it were two different things.

I explained things, at least how I saw things — Kia thinking she was better than me — and then my mother took Kia's side. She finally said that, if she'd known this was going to cause problems between me and Kia, she never, ever would have encouraged us to try out for the team. That was just what I needed. Now nobody, including my mother or Kia, wanted me on the team.

I'd waited for Kia to call on me to go to school this morning. Like I did every school day. She didn't show up on time. I even waited an extra five minutes before I left on my own. It was strange walking by myself, but I guess it could be good practice.

I might be walking alone a lot over the next few weeks. Either because Kia made the team and I didn't, or because I made the team and she didn't. Neither way would be very good, although I knew which one would be worse.

I slowed down as I saw the school in the distance. I felt very alone as I walked through the schoolyard. There were lots of kids out, playing, standing, skipping, kicking a ball around in the field. I didn't see Kia anywhere — not that I was looking for her.

I came up to the doors closest to the gym and froze. Inside, on the wall by the gym, the team list would be posted. I suddenly felt trapped. I couldn't go back home, and I didn't want to go forward. What if my name wasn't on the list? What if Kia's was? What if neither of us made the team? What if I made the team … with or without Roy? I strained to think of a possibility that would be good, and couldn't think of one. But I did know that I couldn't just stand here all day. I took a deep breath and pulled the door open.

The halls were still relatively kid-free. A couple of teachers were standing at the doors of their rooms, coffee cups in hand, talking, and some radio station was playing over the P.A. Up ahead I could see kids clustered together beside the doors to the gym. I saw Kia partially hidden behind the bigger grade five students.

Kia came toward me and stopped.

"I wasn't right," she said.

"You weren't?" Did that mean that I'd made the team and she hadn't?

"Yes. I had it figured wrong." She paused. "We both made the team!"

"Are you sure?"

"I can read, you know!"

"I didn't mean that … I just mean …," I paused and looked down at the ground. "Maybe I shouldn't have … you know … when we were … on Friday."

"Me too," she said. "I was just … I'm really … you know … too."

"Let's just forget it," I said.

"Already forgotten. Do you want to know who else is on the team?"

"Yeah, definitely!"

"Everybody we talked about on Friday except for Scott."

"You mean Roy is on the team?" I said loudly.

"Yeah, he made the —"

"Are you surprised by that?"

I knew without looking around that the voice was Roy's and he was standing right behind me. Slowly I turned around.

"So are you surprised that I'm on the team?" he demanded again.

"No … I'm just …"

"We figured you'd be on the team," Kia said, stepping in to fill my silence.

"You did?" Roy asked. Now he sounded surprised.

"We were talking about it on Friday. We thought you'd be on the team, but we weren't so sure we'd be there on the list as well," Kia continued.

Roy now looked even more confused.

"So I guess that makes us teammates," Kia said.

"Nope," Roy said, moving right in my face. "It's like I said to you before. Just because we're on the same team don't make us teammates."

Roy brushed against me as he moved off down the hall toward the doors.

"I guess he's still being honest," I said after I was sure he was a safe distance away.

"He might learn to —"

"Nice going, guys," Marcus said.

"Thanks," I said.

"Does this mean you can talk to us now?" Kia asked.

Marcus shrugged. "I guess I can talk to my teammates. See you later ... at practice after school."

★★★

"Congratulations!" Mrs. Orr said as we walking into the room.

We were the first two in the class. Everybody else was still waiting outside in the line. We came straight from the gym when we heard the bell, like we had every day this week.

"Thanks," Kia said. "You already knew?"

"I've known since Friday. Mr. Roberts discussed his choices with all the teachers on Friday to make sure we were still in approval with you being part of the team."

"Oh, okay," I said. If I had known on Friday it would have saved me and Kia a big fight, and me two bad nights' sleep.

"He said that as far as he knows you are

the first grade threes to ever make a school team in anything. You must be very proud of your accomplishment."

"Yeah, I guess," I said.

"You sound like you're not so sure about it," Mrs. Orr said. "Aren't you happy?"

"I'm happy."

"Yeah, we're very happy," Kia added.

I turned and went to hang up my backpack. Happy didn't really describe how I felt. It was more like ... like ... like I'd been swimming and I'd dived down really deep to get something, and as I was coming up and up and up and up, trying to reach the surface, I was afraid that I'd run out of air. And then finally, I burst through and took a deep breath of air. It wasn't happy. It was relief. Like I was able to breathe again. It wasn't nearly as good making the team as it would have been bad if I didn't.

"And because you made the team I'll be assigning you two extra homework tonight," Mrs. Orr said.

"You'll be what?" Kia questioned, like she couldn't believe what she'd just heard.

"Extra homework."

"But, but ... that's not fair!" Kia protested.

Mrs. Orr furrowed her brow like she was thinking extra hard. "It most certainly is fair. You two will have to make up for the school time you're going to missing tomorrow."

"Why will we be missing school?" I asked.

"We haven't been late since that first time and we won't be, we promise!" Kia pleaded.

"And I appreciate that. But that's not why you'll be missing school tomorrow. You won't be coming back to class after afternoon recess."

"We won't?"

"Your entire team will be excused for the last part of the day," Mrs. Orr said.

"We have extra practice?" I asked.

"In a manner of sorts. Apparently the team will be going to another school for an exhibition game."

"Fantastic!" Kia exclaimed.

I nodded my head in agreement. I had lots of things going through my mind, none of which had the word 'fantastic' attached to them. At least there'd only be one night to worry about what might go wrong.

# Chapter 9
# The Agony of Defeat

Mr. Roberts changed gears again and the car jolted forward, bouncing me against the seat as it rocked and bumped. Every time he changed gears it registered deep down in the pit of my stomach, which wasn't feeling that great even before we started this trip.

My worst fear was that I'd get sick. Mr. Roberts wasn't the best driver in the world, but his driving couldn't explain my stomach. I was nervous … no, I was more than nervous … I was scared. And there was neither the time nor the place to get sick. I was wedged into the back, my body pressed against one of the other two people who shared the back seat. One of those was Roy. At least I was separated from him by another kid and I didn't have to have to be squished against him.

As we'd gotten into the car he'd made a joke about me. He said how 'lucky' they all were to have me in the car with them because 'a real-sized kid' wouldn't have fit. He certainly did know how to make somebody feel special.

Up ahead through the front windshield I could see Mr. White's car. He and a parent who had volunteered to drive were bringing the rest of the team. I wondered if either of them drove any better than Mr. Roberts and if I could drive back with one of them after the game. Then again, after the game I was sure my stomach was going to be better no matter who was driving.

"So how are people feeling?" Mr. Roberts asked.

"Fine — cool — excited" were the words that bounced back at him. I thought that 'about to bring up' didn't quite fit in.

"The team we're playing today is Vista Heights Public School," Mr. Roberts said.

"Vista Heights!" I exclaimed. "Didn't they win the league championship last year?"

"Yes, they did," Mr. Roberts confirmed. "But all those kids from last year's championship team have graduated and moved on."

That was good to hear. Maybe this year's players wouldn't be as good as last —

"Of course, they've won the league championship four of the last five years," Mr. Roberts added. "They seem to be able to put together great teams year after year."

Everybody in the whole car fell silent. I had a thought that maybe I wasn't the only one who suddenly didn't feel so good.

"I know their coach," Mr. Roberts said. "That's how I was able to arrange this game before the season officially started. You know, have a little friendly game. He said his team wasn't quite up to the standards he expected."

So maybe this wouldn't be so bad after all.

"But I'm sure their coach was just saying that about his team to get me all psyched out. You know, claiming they weren't so good to get us overconfident."

I almost laughed out loud. Being overconfident was just about the last thing I was worried about. The car lurched again and I remembered what I *was* most worried about — barfing in the back seat.

★★★

I tried to stay close to Mr. Roberts as we walked in. Nobody was saying anything. Maybe I wasn't the only one who was feeling nervous. The only sound was the noise of our feet shuffling up the hall.

Then, faintly at first, I could hear the unmistakable sound of basketballs bouncing. We followed the sounds, getting louder and louder. Then I picked up that other basketball sound — the squeaks of sneakers against floor. I loved that sound.

Mr. Roberts pulled open one of a pair of double doors. "Here we are," he said as he ushered us in.

"Wow," somebody mumbled.

Stretched out before us was a gigantic, gleaming gymnasium. It had to be three times as big as our little gym. There were nets — I counted them — eight nets, and bleachers — real live bleachers. I'd played in gyms like this before, when our rep team was in tournaments, but those were always in high schools or colleges or fancy recreation centers. Not ever in elementary schools.

At the far end of the gym, warming up,

was our opposition. They were doing a simple lay-up drill. Simple, but they were doing it well. Very well.

"Okay, everybody, go and get changed," Mr. Roberts said.

Mr. White led us to a bench off to the side, while Mr. Roberts went down to see the teacher leading the drills at the other end. I watched as I walked. The two of them met, shook hands and began joking around, laughing. I turned my attention to the kids doing the drill. Their coach wasn't watching and they still executed the drill perfectly. That wasn't good.

"Here you go," Mr. White said.

"Thanks," I said as I took the sweater he offered me from the bag he was carrying.

I held it up. It was Clark colors — yellow and blue. Number eleven was on the back. These were our school's basketball sweaters. And soccer sweaters, and volleyball sweaters and baseball sweaters. I figured if we had a swim team they would have put these on before they jumped into the pool.

As I slipped it on over top of my T-shirt I caught a deep whiff of the sweater. I didn't think it had been washed for a long time, if ever.

Next I pulled off my tear-aways and sat down to change shoes. Mr. Roberts came back to join us.

"We're going to be starting in a couple of minutes. I want everybody to go out and warm up. Come on, Nick, get those shoes on!"

I did up the laces as quickly as I could, but was still the last on the floor. Kids took shots and fooled around on their own until Mr. Roberts joined us on the floor and set us up to do a lay-up drill. Thank goodness he hadn't asked us to do a weave. That would have been embarrassing.

Between my turns I looked down at the other team. They didn't look much bigger than us. Actually, except for me and Kia, I thought we were probably a little bit bigger.

They'd switched to another drill. They were coming toward the hoop, stopping, and putting up a jumper. They were making some and missing some. Nothing too special.

What was special though was the way they were dressed. They were all wearing basketball sweaters — real basketball sweaters. Gold and black with a gigantic eagle emblem on the front. And they were wearing matching shorts and socks. The only difference between players was their shoes. With us, the only thing the same was our smelly sweaters.

"Come on, Nick, it's your turn," Dean said, handing me a ball.

I dribbled, put a pass over to the other lane, ran to the net to receive the return pass, grabbed the ball and laid it up on the boards for a basket. At least that still worked. Maybe we'd do okay.

"Nice game," he said as he slapped my hand on the way by.

"Nice game," said the second player and then the third and fourth as we walked through the line.

It didn't matter what words came out of their mouths, I could tell by the smirks on their face, and the numbers on the scoreboard, what they really were thinking: you guys stink, you guys suck, you don't belong in the same gym with us. And the worst part was they were right.

The scorekeeper flipped the board back to zero. Thank goodness I didn't have to look at the score any longer. Not that I'd ever forget it. Seventy-six to twenty-nine.

"I want everybody to sit down and we'll talk for a little while before we drive home," Mr. Roberts said.

He was trying to sound cheerful, but I could tell by the catch in his voice that he was as bothered by the score as the rest of us. He was trying his best to hide his feelings.

"Obviously we didn't win today, but we did learn some important things."

I had to agree. We'd learned lots of things — none of which I wanted to know.

"Our challenge is to look at our game, as a team and individually, and decide what we did right and what we need to improve on."

It wouldn't take long to think about what we'd done right. We hadn't scored on our own net, nobody had died, and we'd found the school. That was about it.

There wasn't much for me to do about the way I'd played either. I'd been out for about thirty seconds in the first half and no more than two minutes in the second. I'd taken no shots, made no points, had no fouls, no assists, no rebounds, and had made one steal. That one steal was the only thing separating me from a perfect 'O-fer' game.

"You have to realized that this team we were playing has been together for a long time. They were playing as a group last year," Mr. Roberts said. "Vista always has a 'B' team of grade fours. They practiced with the grade five championship team from last year. So keep in mind that we lost to a very good team."

"Why did we have to play against them for our first game?" Dean questioned, asking the question that I think was on everybody's mind.

"To see what we could do well, and to figure out what we needed to work on. This was a good loss," Mr. Roberts said.

If this was a good loss, I would have hated to see what a bad loss looked like.

"We now have a week to work and improve before we play our first official game of the season. I know where we stand. We'll be working hard to improve certain areas of the game. Any questions?"

Everybody just sat there silently, although I was sure there were things people wanted to ask or say.

"Everybody take off your sweaters," Mr. Roberts said.

I took a deep breath and pulled mine

over my head. At least I didn't have to worry about it being wet from my sweat.

"Do we have a volunteer to take the sweaters home and put them through a wash?" Mr. Roberts asked.

Nobody put up their hand.

"Come on, they really stink," he said.

"Maybe Kia should take them," Roy said.

"I guess I could —," she started to say.

"Because washing is woman's work," he said, cutting her off.

Mr. Roberts shot Roy a nasty look. Saying something like that when a teacher was already angry was not the smartest thing in the world. But then again, look who said it.

"Kia's not going to wash them," Marcus said, jumping in. "And neither is anybody else on this team."

What did he mean … was he wanting one of the coaches to wash them?

"These sweaters stink," he said. "And so do we."

"Marcus we weren't that —"

"Yes, we were!" he exclaimed, cutting Mr. Roberts off. "Look at the score. We stunk today."

Nobody offered an argument.

"We stunk as bad as these sweaters, and I don't think we should wash the sweaters until we stop stinking," Marcus continued.

"You mean, like a protest," Kia said.

Marcus nodded his head. "When we stop stinking, then the sweaters can stop stinking."

A couple of kids nodded their head in agreement.

"Is that what people want?" Mr. Roberts asked.

A few more mumbled or nodded agreement. What he was saying made sense to me — strange, smelly sense, but sense.

"Then that's it," Mr. Roberts said. "The sweaters don't get washed until we show we can play better. Stuff 'em in my bag and I'll hang onto them for the next game."

# Chapter 10
# Using Your Head

I took a long swig from my water bottle. It was amazing how sitting on a bench could work up a thirst.

The game was more than three-quarters over and the only time either Kia or I had been on the floor was during the warm-ups.

And it wasn't like having us out there would cost us the game. We were down by almost thirty points.

"Do you think we're going to get on at all?" I whispered to Kia who was sitting beside me on the bench.

She shrugged. "Hey, Mr. Roberts," Kia said loudly, "are you going to play us or what?"

"Later in the game, Kia," he said, without turning his attention away from the game.

"Later? Like later when?" she asked. "Like if we tie the game up and get into overtime?"

Mr. Roberts let out a loud sigh. "Now's as good a time as any. Nick, and Roy, get ready to go in."

"Roy? What about me?" Kia asked.

"You'll go in when Nick comes out," he answered. "Roy replace Dean, Nick you take out Bojan."

Roy and I went to the scorer's table and crouched down, waiting for the next stoppage in play to get in.

"When we get out there," Roy said to me. "Stay out of my way."

Those weren't exactly the words of encouragement I usually expected from a teammate. I moved slightly away from him as we waited.

On the court Marcus drove for the net and was fouled. I stood up and stretched my legs. The ref would let us sub in after the first throw.

His first shot went up and clanked off the iron, bouncing off to the side. The ref called us in. Roy took a spot on the key, waiting to go for the rebound if Marcus missed his second shot. I stopped at center court, covering the man there.

The shot went up, hit the rim, spun around and then bounced free. A player with a red jersey came up with the ball. He looked up court and reared back, getting ready to toss the ball. I took a quick look over my shoulder — the man I was covering had moved away and was free under our net. I rushed back, trying to look back for the pass I knew was coming. I leaped up just in time to grab the ball, pulling it in. I had it! I planted both feet and then started away, dribbling it back up court. Suddenly I was swarmed by three of their players, just as I reached the half.

I looked between the three of them and caught a glimpse of one of our players alone under their net. I heaved the ball over the outstretched fingers of the charging trio and it landed right where I'd aimed — and prayed — it would go. I lost sight of the player, but saw the ball go up and into the net!

Then I could see him. It was Roy, and he had a smile on his face. That was even rarer than our team scoring a basket. I thought

I detected a slight nod of his head as he passed by me.

The other team quickly came up. The guard came straight up and without looking left or right launched a long three-point shot. It was an air ball which Marcus corralled. He started to dribble and I broke up the side, angling to the corner. I raised my hand to signal I was open. No sooner had that happened than the ball flew through the air and I grabbed it. I started to dribble, driving the net. Out of nowhere my clear lane vanished and two of their players blocked me out. I caught sight of one of our players breaking free on the other side. I bounced a pass to him just as one of their men collided with me, sending me tumbling to the floor.

I heard a cheer go up and scrambled to my feet in time to see Marcus giving Roy a high five. I'd fed Roy another pass and he'd scored again! We were making a run!

I started back up the court, but then spun around quickly as I expected the in-bounds pass to come in. It was going to a man just over from me and I lunged out and grabbed the ball just before it reached him. Without hesitation I drove back toward their basket.

It would be an easy two points.

And then I felt a hard shove to my back and tried to put up my hands to block the rapidly approaching wall and ...

★★★

"Nick can you hear me?"

I felt my head spinning. Who was calling me?

"Nick ... can you hear me?"

It was Mr. Roberts. "Sure ... yeah," I muttered.

"Wonderful ... great ... and do you know where you are?"

What sort of stupid question was that? Of course I knew where I ... I looked around. Where was I? It looked like the little room beside the office ... how did I get here? I remembered being in the gym and going up for a lay-up and then hitting the wall ... and looking up and seeing one of their players standing over top of me — scowling.

"Did I make it?" I asked.

"Make what?" Mr. Roberts asked. He sounded really worried.

"The shot," I mumbled. "Did I score?"

"Yes, you got it!" Kia exclaimed. "And

Marcus took the foul shot and we got the ball back and —"

"But the important thing is that you're okay," Mr. Roberts said, cutting her off.

"Did we win?" I asked.

"We lost," Kia said. "By a lot."

"The only thing that's important is that you're fine. Your mother should be here soon," Mr. Roberts said.

"My mother? Why is my mother coming?"

"We called her. We were very worried, and we want her to take you to see the doctor."

"Why do I have to go and see a doctor?"

"It's just a precaution. We need you to be checked out. You took a very nasty blow to the head."

"I'm fine," I protested.

"I'm sure you are," Mr. Roberts agreed. "But you still have to be examined."

"But I'm okay," I protested. I tried to sit up and suddenly the whole world tilted to the side and my stomach lurched forward. I threw up all over the floor beside the couch. Maybe I wasn't that fine after all.

# Chapter 11
# Back in the Game

"So Nick, how are you doing today?" Mr. Roberts asked.

"I'm fine," I offered, and I *was* feeling fine.

It was strange, but over the past week when people said to me, 'how are you,' they really meant it. I'd missed two days of school. I'd felt kind of weak, and sick to the stomach. When my mom had taken me to the hospital, I'd seen a doctor and he'd told us that I had a 'minor concussion.' If this was minor, I'd hate to ever find out what a major one would feel like.

"Nick, you don't have to come out and

watch us practice," Mr. Roberts said.

"I'm not here to watch, I'm here to practice."

"I don't think that would be wise."

"The doctor said it would be okay," I said, as I pulled a note out of my pocket and handed it to him.

He studied it carefully. "I guess it's okay if the doctor says so. You are feeling better, right?"

"Much better."

"Good. Just take it easy ... nothing too hard."

"I'll be careful."

I walked over to the edge of the stage, where Kia was sitting. Everybody else was putting on their gear on the bench.

"So is he letting you practice?" she asked.

"I'm back." I pulled my shoes out of my bag.

Kia smiled. "It was getting pretty lonely without you. Now at least I'll have somebody to talk to while we watch the games."

She hadn't been on the floor since I was injured. I knew it wasn't my fault, but I still felt responsible. Like if I hadn't had my bell rung, then maybe Mr. Roberts would have felt okay and let her play more. I figured he was afraid she'd get hurt too. I couldn't help but wonder if we'd get much — or any — playing time for the rest of the season.

Mr. Roberts blew his whistle and I quickly tied up the second shoe and jumped off the stage to join the group already assembling around him. I got there just as they started to run laps. I joined the end of the line.

"Come on, let's move it!" Mr. Roberts bellowed. "A winning attitude starts in practice! Pick it up!"

The pace quickened and I found myself starting to struggle to keep up. My head felt better but my legs and lungs weren't there. I puffed and huffed and tried to dig a little bit deeper. Maybe coming back this soon wasn't smart.

"Pick it up!" Mr. Roberts yelled. "Everybody except Nick … you slow it down."

For a split second I felt grateful to slow down until I looked at the expressions of my teammates. They didn't look happy about me receiving special treatment. I was just glad I couldn't read minds … although I knew what most of them were thinking.

★ ★ ★

Sitting on the bench watching us lose was even worse than sitting in the bleachers and watching the same thing. And it wasn't like the game was that interesting. Blow-outs are always boring.

As it got more and more one-sided, I stopped even looking at the score. I stopped looking at the play. Instead I put my eyes elsewhere. At first I looked at the bleachers. I saw the other kids and the teachers and the parents from our side and the other team's parents. Then I saw my father sitting there beside my mother. He'd gotten off work early to see this. Me sitting on the bench in a losing game.

I didn't know, but I thought my mother would be happy that I was on the bench. Not that she'd said anything, but I think she felt some of the same things that Mr. Roberts felt. With me sitting on the bench, she knew I couldn't get hurt. At least if I didn't get a splinter in my butt.

My mother waved and I gave a little wave and then looked away. There had to be some-place else to look. I turned my eyes to the ceiling. I started counting the vents and then tried to figure out how to get down the bean bags and dodge balls which were lodged up there in metal beams.

The final buzzer sounded and disturbed my thoughts. I joined the rest of the team at center court to shake hands with the other team. As I walked out, I realized I didn't even know the final score. But I did know some things: 1) we'd lost, 2) we lost big, 3) we were now 0–4 for the season, 4) neither Kia nor I had played, 5) I didn't think we'd play again this whole season, and 6) there was nothing we could do about any of the above.

I took a deep breath and then quickly pulled my sweater over my head and took it off. I stuffed it into my gym bag and did up the zipper, sealing in the smell. My mother had started to make me keep the bag in the garage. She said it smelled like a small animal had crawled into my bag and died. She was wrong. It smelled like a *big* animal had crawled in and died. I would have liked to have let her wash it, but that smelly sweater seemed like the only thing that I shared with my teammates.

"Well, that was a complete waste of time," I said to Kia.

"Maybe you would have gotten more out of the game if you'd have watched it."

"I watched it ... some of it," I protested.

"I watched all of it. And because I did, I think that I've solved our problems."

"What problems?"

"Boy, you really weren't paying any attention to that game."

"I meant what specific problems did you mean?" I asked.

"The obvious ones. You and I not playing. The team losing. I've got it figured out."

I gave her a questioning look. "And what exactly is the answer, or answers, that you've figured out?"

"I can't tell you. I have to show you."

"Okay, go ahead and show me."

She shook her head. "I can't. Not here and not now."

"Then where and when?"

"Tomorrow, at your house. But first I have to talk to a few other people and convince them to come."

"Who do you have to talk to?"

"Marcus, Kingsley and Roy."

# Chapter 12
# The Plan

I bounced the ball on the driveway. I felt anxious. I looked at my watch. It was almost noon and nobody had shown up yet. Not even Kia. What if nobody but Kia came? No, that didn't make sense; Marcus would come. What if Roy got here before either of those two? What was I going to talk to him about: how much he hated me, and where he'd like to punch me? Actually I didn't know why I was wasting my time thinking about that. Roy had made it pretty clear to Kia that he wasn't coming. He said he had to spent too much time around us during the week, so there was no way in the world he was going to show up at my house on the weekend.

I'd hardly finished my thought when Kia appeared around the corner. She waved and then started to jog.

"Nobody here yet?" she asked.

"Not yet. Maybe not at all."

"They'll be here. At least some of them will be for sure."

"I still don't know why you had to invite Roy. Couldn't you have asked Dean or Bojan or anybody else?"

Kia shook her head. "Roy is the guy. He'll be perfect."

Now it was my turn to shake my head. "Those are two words you don't usually hear in the same sentence — Roy and perfect."

"That depends," Kia said. "What about if the sentence was something like, 'Roy is a perfect jerk'."

I laughed. "So are you going to explain things to me now?"

"Not yet. I hate having to say the same thing twice."

"And I hate waiting."

"Then we're both in luck," she said.

Kia pointed up the street and I turned

around. Marcus, Kingsley *and* Roy were coming down the street. I felt a rush of relief, excitement and dread all rolled into one.

"Hey guys, sorry we're a bit late," Marcus said. Kingsley nodded hello and Roy scowled.

"That's okay. I just got here myself," Kia said.

Marcus looked at me. "Say, Nick ... I was wondering if maybe your mother ..."

"Four dozen," I said.

He smiled.

"Four dozen what?" Kingsley asked.

"Cookies," Marcus said. "Chocolate chip cookies. Nick's mother makes the best cookies in the world."

Roy chuckled. "So you've been coming here with your little buddies for milk and cookies."

"Yeah," Marcus said defiantly, taking a step toward Roy. "You want to make something of it?"

Roy came toward Marcus, but before anybody could say or do anything, Kia stepped between them. I didn't know if that was really brave, or really stupid.

"How about if we make something of this team instead?" she asked.

They both stopped.

"I want to explain to you, to show you how our team can win," she said.

"Our basketball team?" Kingsley asked.

"Of course, our basketball team."

"That would be some trick," Marcus said. "So what have you got in mind?"

"I've been watching our games," she said.

"You've had plenty of time to watch," Roy said, "since that's all you've been doing."

She ignored his shot. "And I think I know how we can win, and I think the five of us are the best people on the team to do it." She paused dramatically, leaving everybody waiting.

"Well?" I finally asked, breaking the silence.

"We need a press ... a full court press."

"A press?" Roy and Kingsley said in unison.

"Full court. I've noticed that none of the teams have a press —"

"That's because it's hard to do right," Marcus explained.

"Hard, but not impossible. And I've also noticed that any time anybody even puts the least bit of pressure on the other team, it really creates trouble."

"Maybe, but what makes you think we

can apply a press?" Kingsley asked.

"We can if we practice," Kia argued.

"And Mr. Roberts has agreed to this?" Marcus questioned.

"No. I thought that before we told him about it we should do some practicing."

"When and where?" Marcus asked.

"Starting today. Here."

"Here!" Roy exclaimed. "You want me to come here and spend even more time with a couple of grade threes?"

"And a couple of grade fives," Kia said, pointing to Kingsley and Marcus.

"What a waste of my time," Roy snapped.

"Why, do you like losing or something?" Kia asked.

"No, I don't like losing, and I wouldn't have to if we didn't have a couple of little kids on our team!"

"And who do you think we have at the school who is better than these two?" Marcus said, gesturing to me and Kia.

"I'm out of here!" Roy snapped.

He started to stomp away when Kingsley grabbed him by the shoulder. "Hang on a second," he said. "I have a question. When the three of you beat us in the three-on-three tournament, did you come here to practice?"

"All the time," Marcus said. "That's how I know about Nick's mother's cookies, and her lasagna and stew too."

"That's the only reason we were able to beat your team. And if we practice the press then maybe, just maybe, our team can win a couple of games," Kia said.

Nobody said anything, not even Roy, but I could tell everybody was thinking about it.

"Okay everybody, I'm going to divide you into two groups and we'll scrimmage," Mr. Roberts said.

I looked at Marcus, who nodded at Kingsley, who was looking at Roy.

"This is the time," Kia said as she tapped me on the arm. We all knew what we had to do. If we could get on the same side, we could try the press and show it to Mr. Roberts.

We'd practiced it for hours on Saturday and then on Sunday for another three hours. We'd been at my house so long that first day that my father ordered pizza for the five of us for supper, and we all sat around on the porch munching it.

Mr. Roberts started to toss out the red bibs. The five players who received them would be on the same side against the remaining five. We had to be on the same side.

Marcus, Kingsley and Kia were among those who got the bibs. I looked at Roy and shrugged. He scowled back. He then walked over to Bojan, who had received a bib, said something to him I couldn't hear, and Bojan handed the bib to him. Roy turned my way and pitched me the bib. I slipped it on over my head. Roy approached another player with a bib and took that one from him, putting it on over his jersey.

"Okay everybody, let's ...," Mr. Roberts stopped mid-sentence. "These aren't the teams I selected."

"We just wanted to try something different," Kia said.

"How about if we just do what I want to do since I'm the coach."

"I know, sir, it's just —"

"We thought it would be good for me to be out on the same line as Kia and Nick," Roy said, cutting her off. "You know I'm pretty big and I can help take care of them so nobody pushes them around too much."

"You want to take care of them?" Mr. Roberts questioned. His tone of voice and expression left little doubt he was pretty surprised by Roy's statement.

"Yeah. Why wouldn't I want to take care of one of my teammates?"

"Well ... sure ... I guess we could try this line combination for a little bit ... in practice," Mr. Roberts said.

That's what I wanted to hear.

"We'll even give them first ball," Roy offered.

This may have sounded like a nice offer, but it was just what we wanted — them with the ball to in-bounds.

Roy picked up the ball and slowly rolled it down to the baseline. He then took up a position directly in front of Dean, who was going to throw the ball in. Roy began jumping up and down, waving his arms in the air like he was going to try to fly.

Marcus and I took up our positions. We sandwiched Bojan between us.

"What are you guys doing?" Bojan asked.

"It's called coverage," Marcus said. "Coverage like a blanket."

Without looking away from Bojan I knew

where Kia and Kingsley were — Kia just on this side of center and Kingsley just a little bit on the other side.

"Come on, you going to throw in the ball or try to hatch it?" Roy demanded. "You only have five seconds you know ... that's the rules ... come on!"

"But I can't —"

"One ... two ... three," Roy started to count.

Dean tried to move out of Roy's way and tossed in the pass. It just deflected off one of Roy's outstretched arms and bounced off target. Marcus and Bojan scrambled after it. Marcus got the ball and fed it to me. Dean came toward me and I lobbed it over to Roy who was under the net, alone. He put it up for an easy two points.

I heard Kia whoop and turned around to see her giving Kingsley a high five.

Roy picked up the ball and handed it to Dean. "Try it again," he said.

Before Dean could even get ready to toss it in, we were back all over Bojan again. He jumped and dodged and spun and turned to try to get away from us. The ball came in to the left just as he spun to the right. It shot pass all three of us and was grabbed by Kia. She instantly fed the ball over to me and I sent it to Marcus as he broke for the net. Another easy two points!

"Somebody come back and help!" Dean yelled as he picked up the ball.

Nobody moved.

"Give him some support!" Mr. Roberts yelled. "They're putting on a press!"

Two of their guys came back to give Dean a target. Kia came back with them and Kingsley moved up to take the spot she'd occupied. Marcus and I slipped away from Bojan, getting ready to get on whoever received the pass.

Dean looked one way, and then the other as his players yelled and waved and dodged around trying to get open.

He threw it to Scott. Kia and Marcus were closest to him and they collapsed on him, forcing him to go to the sidelines, where they trapped him. He turned and thought about throwing it back to Dean, but he was being pushed to the side by Roy. In desperation he just tossed the ball over top of Marcus. Kingsley grabbed the lame throw and he fed it into me. I put up a short jumper and it went into the net!

This wasn't going as we planned ... it was even better!

Mr. Roberts blew his whistle and we stopped. "Okay, everybody, bring it in!" he yelled.

I fought hard not to let out a little yell — a victory yell. Marcus, Kingsley, Kia and even Roy were all smiling. But why shouldn't they? We were amazing!

"Let's talk about what happened," Mr. Roberts called out.

It seemed like it was pretty obvious what had happened. We hadn't just beaten the other guys, we'd buried them. Every single time they'd tried to bring it up we'd stopped them and put it back in their net.

We all settled onto the bench in front of Mr. Roberts.

"You wanted to try something a little different," Mr. Roberts said to us.

"Did you like it?" Kia asked.

"I hated it!" Dean said.

"Yeah, they were driving me crazy!" Bojan added and Mohammed nodded his head in agreement.

"You five have obviously been practicing," Mr. Roberts said.

"Not that much," Marcus said. "Just this

weekend for a few hours."

"On both Saturday and Sunday," Kia added.

"We worked hard. It's not that easy," I said.

Kia and I had agreed that the worst thing was to do all this work and then have Mr. Roberts put two other players out there instead of us and have us sit on the bench.

"Who's idea was this?" Mr. Roberts asked.

"Kia's," Marcus said. "She had the idea, asked us to come over, and then convinced us that it would work."

"She's convinced me!" Dean said. "Can the rest of us learn how to do it?"

"It's not that hard," I said.

"But it takes time, so we couldn't show you before tomorrow's game," Kia added.

Mr. Roberts didn't say anything. He knew she was right. It wasn't possible to teach anybody enough to take my place or Kia's. Either he was going to play us and we'd help to put the press into place, or he wouldn't and there wouldn't be a press. The question was whether he was tired enough of losing to risk putting Kia and me back in the game.

# Chapter 13
# Full Court Press

I heaved up a shot at the net. The ball missed by a mile. Maybe my eyes were on the hoop, but my mind was elsewhere. I was wondering what Mr. Roberts would do. Or I guess let us do. Would he let the five of us play the press? Would he even let Kia and me on the floor?

The ref whistled to signal the game would start in two minutes, and Mr. Roberts waved us to the bench.

We all took seats on the bench and Mr. Roberts paced in front of us.

"Our opponents have played five games. They've lost four and won only the one game.

They're not that good," he said.

If they weren't very good and had won one more game than us, then what did that make us?

"This is a winnable game. I want us to go out there and give it our best shot. And if we do that, even if we lose we can still walk out with our heads high."

That wasn't exactly the inspirational pre-game talk I'd been hoping for. Basically he was saying that we were not very good, but they weren't very good either, so because of that we had a slight chance of winning — but if we didn't win, it would be okay.

At least this game was being played at another school. Usually you were supposed to like playing at home, in front of the kids from your school. That had just been embarrassing. It was better to lose in front of strangers and then walk away, hoping you'd never have to see them again.

The ref blew his whistle again. It was game time.

"Okay everybody, listen up. Start off we're going to go with Marcus, Kingsley, Dean, Mohammed and Bojan. Go out there and play!"

The five of them stood up. Marcus looked at me, shrugged, and gave me a 'what can you do about it' sort of look.

Roy shifted down the bench until he was right tight beside me. I had a rush of fear and had to fight the urge to quickly move away.

"Don't worry," he said quietly. "He wants to see what the other team looks like before he puts us out as a unit."

"You really think so?"

"If he doesn't, then maybe we have to try and convince him. Besides, who knows, maybe we don't need the press for this —"

Roy stopped as the other team came down and scored the first basket of the game.

★★★

"This isn't too bad at all," Mr. Roberts said.

What game was he watching, I wondered. It was half-time and we were down twenty-seven to seventeen.

"This is the closest we've ever been at half-time before," he continued.

"Great, so we have our closest loss of the season," Roy grumbled.

"With that attitude we don't have a chance

at winning," Mr. Roberts said.

"It's not my *attitude* that's the problem!" Roy snapped.

"I don't think that's a fair statement to make, Roy," Mr. Roberts said. "We've been losing, but I don't think any of your teammates have given up."

"I'm not talking about my teammates or *their* attitude. I'm talking about you."

There was stunned silence. Nobody said a word. Nobody seemed to even breath.

"We can beat this team," Roy said. "If you let us."

"He's right, sir," Marcus agreed.

"Let us put on the press," Kia said.

"Just to see if it works," I added.

"The press would work," Dean chipped in.

"Give it a chance," Rajinder agreed and everybody else nodded their heads in agreement.

"And if it doesn't work, then we shut up. All of us," Roy said.

We all sat there, waiting for Mr. Roberts to say something ... anything. He looked like he was thinking. That was a good sign. Unless he was thinking we were a bunch of rude kids who he didn't want to coach anymore.

"I've already listed the starting five on my clipboard," he said quietly, tapping the board with his finger. "And nothing that you've said has changed my mind in the least about that."

He weren't going to let us play — everything that was said was for nothing.

"That isn't —"

"Button it!" Mr. Roberts said, cutting Roy off. "And here are the starting five for the next half," he said, turning the clipboard so we could see it. In big red letters were the names Marcus, Kingsley, Roy, Nick and Kia.

He was going to play us all along!

"Now let's get out there and play!"

We got up and everybody cheered and screamed, the sound echoing off the walls of the change room as we ran out the door and into the gym. The other team had been warming up already, but they all stopped and stared as we came out yelling.

It was the other team's ball to start the second half. As I walked up court to take up my position, I felt that strange sensation in the pit of my stomach that had been missing when I knew I wasn't going to play. It was a cross between that feeling you get Christmas morning as you're running down the stairs to open your presents, and the feeling you get while sitting in the waiting room at the dentist's, and hearing the drill going in the other room.

"Let's get 'em," Marcus said as he walked over and gave me a low five.

The ref gave the ball to their throw-in man. They weren't reacting to what we were doing at all. One man was back to take the in-bounds pass, while the other three were far up court. I could just barely see their player, hidden behind Roy.

"Come on, ref, he's only got five seconds to throw it in!" Roy bellowed.

The player we were covering hardly moved. It was like he didn't understand any of what was happening.

"Come on, move! Get open!" the throw-in player screamed.

The ref blew his whistle. "Time violation. Ball turns over to Clark!"

Roy stepped out of bounds, took the ball from the surprised player and then tossed it to the ref. The ref immediately handed it back to Roy who instantly passed it in to Marcus. Before the other team could even think to react, he put up an easy two-pointer and I heard our entire bench scream out!

Nobody on the floor made a sound though. We'd agreed that we wouldn't congratulate ourselves or lose our focus after the baskets. We were just going to get more and more intense each time we scored or stole the ball. More intense, more serious ... more scary.

Their man took the ball from the ref and got ready to in-bounds it again. The ball was hardly in his hands when he threw out a wild pass. Marcus gobbled it up, passed over to me, and I completed a pass to Roy who was right underneath, uncovered. He put it up and in!

Suddenly it was twenty-seven to twenty-one. This game wasn't just in reach. It was in the bag.

★★★

We all hooted and hollered as we ran into the change room. The final score was forty-three to thirty-seven. Not only had we won, we'd limited them to ten points in the whole second half!

They were so frustrated that in the end

they'd started pushing and shoving us. That didn't go on for long though. One of their players had stuck out a leg to trip me as I went to go by him. I went crashing to the floor. Roy went right over to that player and stood right beside him. I couldn't hear what he said — nobody could because that was the way Roy would have wanted it — but the player came right over and apologized to me. Maybe Roy could still be a scary jerk, but now he was a scary jerk who was on *my* side.

We'd played almost the whole third quarter and then Mr. Roberts had put out the other five. That was good because we were starting to get tired. He'd put us back out a few minutes into the fourth and we played until the game was pretty well decided.

"Congratulations!" Mr. Roberts said loudly. "We are no longer the last-placed team in the league. We are tied for last place!"

Another cheer went up. I couldn't believe how excited everybody was ... I couldn't believe how excited I was!

"Actually we're not in last," Kia said. "Technically, because we *beat* the team we're tied with, we're ahead of them."

"All right!" Roy screamed out. "We're number eight! We're number eight!"

Everybody started chanting. Mr. Roberts even chanted along in his loud, rumbly voice. Finally he stood up and raised his hands above his head to silence us.

"We have two things we have to take care of. First, I'd like to present the game ball to the player of the game."

"We have a player of the game?" Kingsley asked.

"We've never done it before because I didn't think we necessarily had one before," Mr. Roberts explained.

He walked over and handed the ball to Kia. "Congratulations on being the player who used her brains as well as her abilities to turn things around."

The whole team cheered. That somehow seemed almost more amazing than our win. Who would have predicted this happening a week ago?

"And the second matter," Mr. Roberts continued. "Can everybody please leave me their sweaters. Now that we don't stink anymore, it's time that the sweaters didn't stink anymore."

# Chapter 14
# Another 'W'

"And just before we conclude our morning announcements," Ms. Grieve said over the P.A., "I'd like to make note of our school basketball team. They did us proud last night with their third-straight win of the season, leaving them in fifth place in the league! Let's give them a big round of applause!"

Everybody in the class started to cheer. I felt myself start to blush. I remembered that my grandmother once said to me that blushing was happiness rushing to get out. That thought made me blush more.

"Have another great Clark day!" Ms. Grieve said as she ended the announcements.

"Kia and Nick, I was wondering, how much longer there is to go in the season?" Mrs. Orr asked.

"One more game," I said.

"Unless we make the playoffs," Kia added.

"I didn't know there were playoffs," Mrs. Orr said.

"Oh, for sure. The top four teams make the playoffs," Kia said.

"But we're not in fourth right now," I said.

"Right now," Kia agreed. "But we could be in fourth if we win our last game."

"If we win our last game and the team that's already in fourth place *loses* its last game," I added.

"Then we'd both be tied with four wins and four losses, but we'd get in because we beat them when we played," Kia explained.

"So you still have a chance," Mrs. Orr said.

"Not much of one. They're playing the last-place team in the whole league. They've only won one game this season," I said.

"Maybe that team has gotten better," Mrs. Orr said encouragingly.

"Not likely," I answered.

"Didn't your team suddenly get better?" she asked.

"I'm sure nobody expected your team to have a chance to qualify for the playoffs after your first few games of the season."

"I guess you're right," I admitted.

"And if you surprised a lot of people, maybe that team will surprise you," she continued.

"That would be nice."

"That's a more positive attitude. Now I'd like everybody to open up their reading books. I'd like to start the day with silent reading."

A little cheer went up from the class as everybody dug into their desks to get their books. Everybody loved silent reading, including me. There always seemed to be so many good books to read. I pulled out my book and opened it up to the spot where I'd left my book mark.

The novel was called *Silverwing* and it was about bats. Normally I'm not into stories with talking animals, but there was something about this book that I really liked.

I was just about to start reading when I began to think about what Mrs. Orr had said. She was right, our team really had improved and it wasn't just because of the press. That had just been the beginning. Using the press had allowed us to score some points and that started us winning and that started us believing that we actually could win.

All the things that Mr. Roberts had been teaching us in practice seemed to start working. People were passing more, and setting picks. And suddenly things like our free throws started to drop, and people were running back faster on defense, and getting rebounds, and when a ball was loose our players would throw themselves on the floor to get it.

Of course, it hadn't hurt that we'd all kept doing extra practice. Every lunch and every recess the ten of us would get together on the court in our schoolyard. Ms. Grieve had given us special permission so we could have the court all to ourselves until the end of the season.

And practice didn't end there. Kids from the team, and not just the four who had first come to my house, were over at my place. Some evenings and every weekend there were people from the team on my driveway, playing, practicing and just fooling around with the ball.

I knew my father *loved* this. Sometimes he'd come out and watch us. A couple of

times he even played. He wasn't bad for a guy his age — after all he had just turned forty-three.

Stranger though was what I believed my mother thought about all those kids being over and all that basketball being played. She loved it even more than my father! I even thought she was starting to understand the game. She was always out offering people something to drink, or treats, and she invited kids to stay for meals. Even Roy.

That first time Roy stayed for dinner — along with Marcus — I wasn't sure what surprised me the most: what good manners he had, or the fact that he out-ate my father. I'd never seen anybody even come close to putting away as much food as him.

Actually the thing that completely shocked me more anything was the fact that Roy and I had become friends. Maybe not friends like I was with Kia, or even like I was with Marcus, but we were friends.

You had to understand Roy, though, to know that he always was going to treat people a certain way. He still insulted, snarled, scowled, snapped and called me names. But between those things he'd do something nice, or smile or be friendly. That was just how he was. Not just with me, but with everybody. That was his way of being friendly.

"All right, everybody, let's finish it up!" Mrs. Orr announced. "Please mark in your journals the pages you've read today and make a short entry to describe your reading."

I closed my book and dug into my desk to find my journal. This was going to be one short journal entry: read from the top of page 93 to the top of page 93. Maybe I better put down a couple more pages than that. I could skip back later and read the pages I'd written I already read and maybe I could say something like, 'and the bats continued their journey,' in my journal.

We all quietly changed out of our sweaters and into our street sneakers. We'd done all we could do. We'd won our last game of the season.

I knew there were times when my head hadn't been into the game. Part of my mind was elsewhere, thinking about a gym on the other side of the city where two other teams were playing. Winning didn't matter at all unless there was a loss to go along with it someplace else.

"We did what we had to do," Mr. Roberts said.

Everybody nodded or mumbled in agreement.

"All we can do is go home, get a good night's sleep and come back tomorrow morning."

"Is there a practice tomorrow?" Kia asked.

Mr. Roberts shrugged. "I guess we'll schedule it, but we can't be sure until we know what happened with the other game, and we won't know that until tomorrow."

There was a knock on the door of the change room and Ms. Grieve walked into the room.

"Ms. Grieve, this is the boys' change room!" Roy protested.

"I figured since Kia was in here there wasn't much danger in me coming in." She chuckled. "I thought you might like to hear some news ... I just got a phone call ... you're in the playoffs."

# Chapter 15
# The Semi's

"Nick, are you still awake?"

I sat up in bed at the sound of my father's voice.

"You should really try to get to sleep," he said.

"I've been trying. I just haven't been succeeding."

He sat down on the edge of my bed. "You're just like I used to be before a big game. I'd be awake thinking through the game and —"

"All the things that could happen," I said, finishing his sentence.

He nodded his head. "I'm still the same way before a big presentation at work."

"Great," I muttered. "I thought I'd out-grow it eventually."

My father chuckled. "Didn't happen for me, but you never know. Your team finished fourth, right?"

"Yep."

"So is your game tomorrow against the team that finished first or second?"

"Second place."

"That's good ... isn't it?"

"Very good. The first-place team beat us once during the season and once in an exhibition game and they were undefeated for the whole season. There wasn't one team that got within fifteen points of them."

"That's great," my father said.

"Maybe for them."

"No, for your team."

"How do you figure that?" I asked.

"If they've always won by a lot, then they won't know how to handle a close game."

"They didn't look like they'd be panicking much," I said, recalling how cool they were. "And, besides somebody would have to make it close to find out if they'd panic."

"I see." He paused. "And the team you're going to play tomorrow, what are they like?"

"They're good. They beat us and only lost two games all season."

What I didn't say was that they were also the team that we were playing when I was bounced into the wall and out of the game. I'd thought a lot about facing them again.

"And do you think you can take them?" my father asked.

"We have a good shot if we can just keep playing the way we've been playing."

"That's the attitude. Is the game being played in the other school's gym?"

"Yep. They got home-court advantage for finishing ahead of us in the standings. But that's okay with me. It's easier to play when nobody I know is watching us."

"I see," my father said quietly.

Had he been planning on going to the game and I'd chased him away?

"But you can come if you want!" I exclaimed.

"And I'd like to be there, but I can't come tomorrow. I have a work commitment I can't get away from."

"That's too bad," I said.

"When are the finals scheduled?"

"They're on Thursday, right after schoo

"In that case I'll make arrangements to be free for that."

"But what if we don't make it to the finals?"

"Then you and I will go out after school and do something, maybe go to the arcade or play some laser tag or something."

"That would be great."

"And who knows, maybe your team will make it to the finals and the first-place team will be eliminated in their game."

"That's not going to happen," I snorted.

"Then you'll just have to beat them in the finals." He paused. "I guess all this talk isn't helping you get to sleep, is it?"

I nodded my head. He'd just gotten my racing mind going even faster.

"In that case, then why don't you come downstairs for a while," he suggested. "I know just what'll make you feel more tired. We'll get you a big glass of milk and a bowl of cereal, and we'll sit up together and watch a little late night TV."

"That'll make me sleepy?"

"It always works for me. Come on."

I threw off the covers and climbed out f bed.

★★★

On the way to the game I decided that Mr. Roberts' driving had improved during the course of the season. He wasn't rocking and rolling so much. In fact, my stomach felt fine — no, better than fine — there was no hint of nervousness or upset. And it wasn't just me. Everybody in the car was joking and laughing and having a good time. Why was everybody so relaxed? It wasn't like we'd done well against the team we were going to play. They'd beaten us badly. Of course, that was early in the season and we'd improved a whole bunch. Maybe we could take them. Suddenly my stomach did a little flip and I realized why everybody seemed so relaxed about this game. Even if we lost we'd still have gone a lot farther than anybody had thought we would. We had nothing to lose … unfortunately, having nothing to lose meant we probably *would* lose.

Still, it would be nice to win and get to the finals. And once we were there, who knows? Maybe Vista would get eliminated in the other semi-final, or maybe they'd make it but we could still take them and … who was I fooling? Nobody could even come close to beating them. Today's game was simply deciding which team was going to lose to Vista Heights in the finals.

Maybe it would be even better if we did lose today. At least we could probably keep it a close game. That would be better than getting killed in the finals.

Mr. Roberts pulled into the parking lot and into a spot. We tumbled out of the car. It was strange, but as soon as everybody exited the vehicle, it was like all the laughter had been left behind. Everybody was suddenly serious, and I felt my stomach tighten up another notch.

I knew that was good. The few times I'd played when I wasn't feeling nervous I'd played badly. So, judging from the size of the knot in my stomach, I was going to have the best game of my life.

Silently we filed into the school and down the hall. Just beside the gym was a change room marked for our team. We went in.

"Let's get changed and warmed up quickly," Mr. Roberts said.

I sat down beside Roy while Kia took a seat on the far side between Rajinder and Bojan. This is how we'd been sitting for a while. Since we'd become part of the team we didn't need to sit side by side and away from everybody else.

That thought made me feel good.

My mind turned toward the last game we'd played against this team. I didn't even remember the score. Actually, it was a very forgettable game, especially for me. About the last thing I remembered was being bounced into the wall ... and that player looking down at me and smirking. That part I hadn't forgotten.

"Hey," Roy said, poking me in the ribs. "I want to do more than just win today. I want revenge."

"What do you mean?"

"I want to beat them by more points than they beat us by the last time," he said.

"How much was that?" I asked.

"You don't remember?"

"I don't remember much about that whole day," I admitted.

Roy nodded his head. "They won by seventeen points. I guess you also don't remember the number of the guy who rang your bell."

"No ... although I think I remember his face."

"I remember his face, and his number."

"You remember his number?" I asked.

"Of course, I do. You don't forget a dirty shot like that. How are you feeling about playing against that guy?"

"I'm okay," I said.

"We need you to be better than okay," Roy said. He leaned closer to me. "Anybody bothers you out there and I'll take care of things. Understand?"

I nodded. I appreciated what he said, but couldn't bring myself to say anything in reply.

★★★

I tried not to look at the other team as they warmed up, but I couldn't help myself. Usually I liked to check them out, to see what sort of game they had, but this time I found my eyes following the player who had hurt me. Roy had told me he was number four. The same number as me.

That was where the similarity ended. He was much bigger than me. And he didn't look too happy or friendly, and he certainly wasn't in grade three.

"You watching him?" Roy said as he came up beside me.

"I've seen him."

"He's a big goofy-looking guy, isn't he?" Roy asked.

I thought that was pretty funny coming from Roy, but I knew better — a lot better — than to point that out.

"Wait here," Roy said and walked away.

Wait here? What did he think I was going to do, leave the gym and — I stopped mid-thought as Roy walked over center court and right up to the guy who had hurt me.

The kid stopped bouncing his ball and he and Roy started to talk. Roy turned around and pointed right at me, and I recoiled in shock. Then they both started to walk toward me. Now I did want to leave.

"He wants to apologize to you," Roy said.

"Yeah … I'm … you know … really sorry," he mumbled, looking at my feet.

"And it won't happen again, right?" Roy said.

"Um … yeah … it won't happen again."

"Good. Now why don't you go down to your end of the court and let us warm up," Roy suggested.

The kid turned and walked away.

"How did that happen?" I questioned.

"I asked him ... real polite-like, and he agreed."

"And do you think he meant it?"

"The sorry part I'm not so sure about. And to tell you the truth I'm not even sure he meant that 'it won't happen again' part."

"You aren't?" I questioned in shock.

"Nope. The only part I know for sure is if he hurts you again, it will definitely be the *last* time he tries to hurt you. If you understand what I mean."

Of course I did. I knew that threat from the other end.

"'Cause nobody, and I mean nobody, hurts my friends," Roy continued.

"Your friends? Me?"

"Yeah. What did you think you were, you little idiot! Of course, you're my friend! You *are* my friend ... aren't you?"

"Yeah, sure, of course!"

"Good, because believe me, it's a lot better to be my friend than it is to be my enemy." He paused. "But I guess you'd know all about that, wouldn't you?" Roy chuckled and then walked away and started to warm up again.

★★★

The first half went just about exactly the way we'd wanted it to go. They were expecting to beat us as badly as they had the first time, and when we hit them with the press they just folded. At one point we were up by twenty points. They came back a little, but we were still twelve points ahead when the half ended.

At half-time Mr. Roberts said that he would start the press unit again. He said that the first two baskets of this half would set the tone for the rest of the game. Either we'd be up by sixteen and they'd quit, or they'd only be down by eight and we could be in trouble.

They had first ball. That was good … for us. Roy took up his spot, practically standing on top of the player trying to throw in the ball. Marcus and I crowded down low as well to cover the other guard. Suddenly two more men broke back from up-court. Now he had three targets to choose from. Kia was back to offer support as their three players began weaving and cutting to t to free up a man and — *smack!* — I v knocked down to the ground and —

"Offensive charge! Illegal pick!" screamed out the ref.

I started to get up when a hand was offered to me. It was number four from the other side. I hesitated.

"Sorry," he said.

I gave a half smile and started to offer my hand when Roy pushed in and shoved him out of the way.

"Keep your hands off him!" Roy blurted out as he pulled me to my feet.

"Break it up, boys!" the ref said, stepping in between them.

For a split second I thought Roy wasn't going to listen.

"Okay ... sure, ref ... no problem, ref," Roy said as he took the ball.

He walked toward the sidelines. "Seven!" Roy yelled out.

I almost laughed out loud! Seven was a play designed to get me free for a jump shot — get me free by having Roy set a pick for my man — the guy who'd just knocked me down.

The ball came in to Kingsley. He dribbled to the side and then sent the ball to cus in the corner. That was my signal to break. I curved, cutting around Kia and then brushing right by Roy and — I heard the crash from behind, but didn't look back. The ball came to me and I put up a little ten-foot jumper that rattled and rolled around the rim before settling in for a basket!

Now I could look back. Roy was practically standing on top of the man, glowering down at him, still on the ground.

"Press!" Roy screamed out as he stepped over top of the man and got ready to take up his spot.

We scored the first ten points of the second half. After that we just coasted, not trying to run up the score. It wasn't good to rub it in — part of me wanted to do that, but we didn't.

Now for the good part, and the bad part. The good part was telling my parents. The bad part was getting ready to play Vista Heights in the finals.

# Chapter 16
# The Finals

I always thought that the waiting was the hardest part. Now that I was standing here in the Vista Heights gym a couple of minutes before tip-off, I wasn't so sure. It wasn't that the waiting hadn't been hard — I'd had trouble sleeping and concentrating in school and no appetite for three days — it was just that actually playing was going to be even worse. I just knew it.

I could just see the expressions on the faces of the Vista team when we came out of the change room. It was almost like 'what a joke this is going to be.' And I guess they had every right to feel that way.

I looked up at the big electronic score-board that dominated the end wall. It hadn't been turned on when we'd played Vista in the exhibition game. It was a big board. Really big. That way they could all see in really large, bright lights, just how good they were. And how bad we were.

The clock kept ticking down the seconds until the start of the game. Less than two minutes and counting.

The stands — well at least half the stands — were completely packed. Students from their school, along with parents and teachers, packed the side of the gym directly opposite the Vista bench. They were all excited and cheering and waving little homemade signs.

On the other half of the bleachers sat our supporters. They included half a dozen parents, including both my mom and dad and Kia's mother, and a few teachers from the school. Mrs. Orr sat up there, right beside my parents. Just what I needed, her to tell them how my work had been slacking off the last few days. It would improve once this game was over. Everything would get better.

There were lots of empty spaces all around where the Clark supporters sat.

I really shouldn't be complaining, though. I was so happy that this game was being played here and not at our school. It didn't matter that this gave them home-court advantage. They already had all the other advantages anyway. What it meant was that we didn't have to play in front of our entire school, with everybody watching. If losing was bad, losing badly was worse, and losing badly in front of everybody was even worse again. At least this would be all private and then there'd be a little announcement on the P.A. in the morning. Maybe if we lost badly, Ms. Grieve wouldn't even mention the score and just say something about us playing a great game and then losing.

I stopped mid-thought as the doors to the gym opened up and kids started pouring in. How many kids went to this school? Did they all want to crowd in here to see us lose? It seemed like ... I suddenly realized they weren't Vista kids. They were kids from our school! And coming in with them were half of the teachers at our school, led by Ms. Grieve!

As they took up spots on the bleachers, Ms. Grieve came over and stopped by Mr.

Roberts. I drifted over to where they stood.

"Well, I promised you that you'd have some school support," Ms. Grieve said to Mr. Roberts.

"How did all these kids get here?" Mr. Roberts asked.

"I rented a bus and we took anybody who wanted to come," she said.

"But … but I didn't know anything about it," Mr. Roberts sputtered.

"Nobody on your team knew! We wanted it to be a surprise! Are you surprised?"

"Shocked," he answered.

Numb is what I thought, but didn't say a word. If only we could — the buzzer sounded loudly and I almost jumped out of my shoes.

"Bring it in everybody!" Mr. Roberts bellowed. "It's show-time!"

Quickly we all ran to the bench and took places on the pine.

"I want to start with our press unit," Mr. Roberts said.

A little chill ran up my spine. I was starting. That always felt extra special.

"I want to see if we can throw them of their game, maybe grab a few baskets rig up front and —"

"Excuse me." It was the Vista coach. "I just wanted to tell you how pleased I am to see your team here. I have to tell you that this was the *last* team I expected to meet in the finals, and I wanted to congratulate you and your team on having had such a wonderful season!" He smiled and offered his hand to Mr. Roberts.

Mr. Roberts didn't smile back or take his hand. "That's really a nice thought ... but why don't you wait a while ... like sixty minutes or so. You see, our season isn't over quite yet. Now if you'll excuse us, I have to get back to my pre-game talk."

Mr. Roberts turned back around and faced us. The other coach looked shocked, and then annoyed. He quickly walked away.

The ref blew his whistle and the starters stood up to go on the court.

"Wait," Mr. Roberts said. "Did you hear what their coach said? Not just the words, but the tone of his voice?"

Of course I'd heard him. We'd all heard him and knew what he meant.

"Now turn around and look at the expressions on the faces of their players," Mr. Roberts said.

We all did what he asked. There were five players on the floor, waiting for the game to start, and the rest of them were sitting on the bench. Whether they were standing or sitting, they all had two things in common — the same bright, shiny uniforms on their backs, and the same self-satisfied, smug little smiles on their faces.

"They think this game is already over before it's even begun. The only thing they're worrying about is where they're going to put their trophies," Mr. Roberts said.

I could just picture that. Them bringing home their trophies and showing the trophies to all their families and then putting the trophies on the dressers in their rooms, or on the front hall table, or —

"Coming here today, I was just happy to have made it this far," Mr. Roberts said. "I figured that, win or lose, it really didn't matter. And to be honest, I didn't figure we had much chance to win anyway." He paused. "Did anybody else think that way too?"

Slowly and reluctantly I raised my hand. I looked around and saw that everybody else was doing the same.

"Come on, coach, are you going to

out a team?" the ref called out.

"Give us another few seconds!" Mr. Roberts yelled back.

"Hurry it up!"

Mr. Roberts turned back to us. "But now it's not enough ... I'm not happy to just roll over and smile as we lose. I don't know if we're going to win. But what I do know is that I want to give them a game. I want to wipe those smiles off their faces ... let them know they've been in a game. What do you think?"

"I'd like that," Roy said. "A lot."

"Yeah, lets show 'em," Marcus said.

Everybody nodded their heads and agreed. I felt a tingle go up my spine.

"Okay, everybody!" Mr. Roberts yelled. "Let's go and get 'em!"

I ran onto the court along with the rest of the starters. The Clark parents and students screamed and yelled and jumped up and down as we charged out. I couldn't help but notice that the smirks on the starting ve weren't there any more. The way we'd rged out onto the court seemed to have wn them. That was good.

Kingsley moved into the center to take

the tip-off, the rest of us took up positions, setting up against the players we'd be covering. I looked across to where Roy was setting up. He wasn't just beside his man, he was already pushing against him with his body. Way to go, Roy!

The ref tossed the ball into the air and Kingsley went up for it. Their man got higher and tipped the ball back. Another one of their player grabbed it over top of Kia. He quickly pitched the ball to a breaking man — my man! He took the pass and laid it up for the first two points of the game. Their parents let out a cheer.

"Come on, let's get going!" Roy barked.

The ball was thrown in and Marcus took it up the court. He'd hardly taken it over the half when he was attacked by a double team. He threw it over to Kia who quickly passed it to me. I saw Kingsley breaking and fed him a bounce pass. He drove for the net and the ball was stripped from his hands!

Before we could even think to try and set up any sort of press, their man passed it up to a man breaking ahead of everybody. He took the pass on the run and laid it up on the board. It bounced off the ri and missed, but a man following the play grabbed the rebound and put it back up for a basket. Another wave of cheering rolled off the bleachers.

I looked up at the clock. It was four to nothing and less than thirty seconds had passed. At this rate they'd beat us by more than two hundred and forty points ... to nothing. What good was having a full court press if we never scored and they never had to in-bound the ball?

Marcus took the ball and started up court. As he crossed center he was met by his man. And then a second man, the player who had been covering Kia, came over to double-team him. He tried to pass off, but the ball was partially deflected and bounced into the hands of the player who was covering me. I ran after him, but was helpless to stop him as he went down the court and deposited another basket. This was even worse than the last two games we'd played them. This time, for a few brief seconds before the tip-off, I'd actually dreamt that we had a chance.

"Time-out!" Mr. Roberts yelled out and the ref signaled play to stop.

We all started to drag ourselves back to the bench.

"Hurry it up!" Mr. Roberts bellowed, and we picked up the pace.

"This isn't going to happen like this. Here's what we're going to do. Kia will in-bound the ball to Kingsley who will bring the ball up. Marcus, go deep into the right corner. Nick, go with him, but not as deep. Marcus, I want you to scream for the ball, wave your arms, and Kingsley, you fake a throw to him. Nick, your man is cheating to Marcus so, when the throw is faked, he'll go over to help double-team. I want you to break for the net and the ball is really coming to you. Roy is going to set a pick for you. Roy, I don't want you to just slow down his man, I want him to think he's hit a brick wall. Got it?"

Roy smiled. "Got it, boss."

"And everybody else?" he asked.

We all nodded and mumbled agreement.

"Good," Mr. Roberts said. "And right after Nick makes the basket I want to see the press. I don't want them just covered, I want them smothered. Now do it!"

We hurried back out. My legs were light and I felt better. Not good but better. If some body else was being counted on to get this first basket, then I would have felt good.

Marcus set up right in the corner and I was just over from him, closer to the hoop. Roy was almost right in the paint. Kia threw in the ball and Kingsley took control and started to dribble. Marcus screamed for the ball and I felt the hairs on the back of my neck stand up. Just like it was planned, Kingsley faked a baseball pass to Marcus and my man slid over to try to intercept. At that instant I broke for the net, just brushing by Roy. I heard a collision behind me, but couldn't turn around as the ball flew right into my hands! I drove the net and put the ball up and — *whack!* — I was hit from behind, falling to the court!

"Basket counts!" the ref yelled, and cheering filled my ears.

Kia reached down and grabbed my hand, pulling me up. Roy was standing practically on top of a player, the man who probably pushed me, and the guy was backing off.

"One shot," the ref said, handing me the ball.

I had a chance for a three-point play …
ut if I didn't sink it then we couldn't set up

the press. Everybody set up for the free throw.

"Nice and easy," Marcus said.

"Make him pay for being a jerk," Roy said under his breath. He was staring at the player who seemed to be studying the floor.

I bounced the ball twice, picked it up, took a deep breath and bounced it again. The shot went up ... straight in, nothing but net!

"Set up!" Roy screamed, before the ball had even hit the floor.

We scrambled to our positions as the ref handed their man the ball. He looked left and right as the other guard dodged and moved, trying to shake us. No matter which way he turned, one or both of us were all over him. He charged toward the thrower, hoping for a little flick pass and —

"Time violation!" the ref yelled. "You took too long to throw it in. Clark ball!"

The kid's jaw dropped to the floor as Roy stepped over the line and practically ripped the ball from his hands.

"Watch how it's done!" Roy snarled.

He passed the ball to the ref, who gave it back to him. Without a hint of hesitation he passed the ball to Kia, who took barely a second to turn, square to the net and throw up the ball for a three-pointer. It dropped and the game was tied!

"Set up!" Roy screamed and we all responded again.

I couldn't help but look at the look on the face of the player getting ready to throw in the ball. There was no smile, no smirk, no look of self-satisfaction. He just looked scared.

★★★

"Time-out!" Mr. Roberts called, and the ref whistled the play to a stop and we all ran to the bench.

"We have them right where we want them," he said.

I looked past him to the scoreboard. We were down by one point with twelve seconds left in the game.

"We have the ball. We have the last shot. The players who are on the court, are any of you feeling like you need to come out?"

Nobody said a word. There was no way I was going to volunteer to come out even if I had a broken leg. I was staying on. I'd been off for a good stretch in the middle of the second half and I felt like I could still run and run and run. No problem.

"We have one chance for the final shot. I can just make a decision myself, but I want to know what you all think. Who should take the last shot?" Mr. Roberts asked.

There was dead silence. All I knew was that I was certain who I *didn't* want to take the shot — me. Anybody but me would be fine and —

"Kia," Marcus said. "She's been hot, her man is playing off her and she's got a good shot."

"Yeah, Kia," Bojan agreed. Others nodded in along with that thought.

"You okay with that?" Mr. Roberts asked Kia.

"Sure, no problem," she said.

She sounded confident, but that was just Kia. Even if it was the last thing in the world she wanted to do, she'd never let anybody know.

"Okay, we go for it. Nick, in-bounds it to Kingsley. Marcus, set up like the ball is going to go to you down low ... that's what they'll expect. Roy, I want you to set a pick and Kia will get free and take the shot. Any questions?"

There were none.

"Break!"

I walked over to the ref and got the ball. I took a few seconds, waiting, letting everybody else take up their positions. Kingsley broke sharply toward our net, leaving his man behind. I bounced the ball to him and then jumped in, setting a screen for him if he needed it. He cut left and then back to the right, reaching half court. Marcus streaked into the corner, breaking free, his arms up, yelling for the ball! Every eye in the place was drawn to him ... but not mine ... I knew where the ball was really going. Kia broke. Her man didn't even notice her get free. She ran to the far side of the key, less than a dozen feet away from the net. Kingsley fed her the ball and one of their players desperately lunged toward her. She sent up the shot ... it went over the outstretched finger tips of the player ... going up and up and up ... straight for the net ... and ...

# Chapter 17
# Next Time

The game had been over for more than thirty minutes. Nobody had left the change room yet. That was okay. At least it had given Kia a chance to stop crying. I'd never seen her cry like that before. I didn't think I'd ever forget that look on her face as the ball bounced off the rim and into the waiting arms of one of their players and the buzzer sounded, ending the game. There was a rush of screaming and yelling as their parents and students and teachers came streaming off the bleachers and surrounded the team.

Kia held it together for a while. She didn't cry there out on the court. Not while we were shaking hands with the other team. Not while we stood there and received our second-place trophies. Not while we watched them get their trophies. But as soon as we got into the change room, she burst into tears, just bawling. And there was nothing anybody could do. I tried to talk to her, but it wasn't any good.

"Your parents are all waiting out there," Mr. Roberts said. "We have to get going, but before we do, I want to say something."

He started to move around the room and we waited.

"The other team may have scored more points than us, but we didn't lose. They may have gotten the first-place trophies, but we were second to none. And we didn't lose the game as much as we simply ran out of time. There are no losers in this room. Now everybody come here," he said, standing in the middle of the room.

We all got off the benches and came over to where he stood. Kia looked down at the floor as she came forward.

"Now everybody, put your hands into the center," Mr. Roberts said as he extended his hands. Everybody did the same.

"When we walked into this room today, we were a team ... maybe the best team I've ever coached. When we walk out now, we're no longer a team." He paused and I felt the weight of his words. "And I want to say to you ... to all of you ... how very, very proud I am of you." He paused again. "Now for one last time ... break!" he yelled.

"Those who need a ride home, I'll meet you out by my car. As for the others, go out and let your parents show you how proud they are of you too."

Mr. Roberts gathered up his stuff and left the room. Quickly others followed until Kia and I were left alone in the room. She looked like either she hadn't been paying attention to what Mr. Roberts had said or she didn't believe him.

I got up and walked toward her. "Come on, Kia, it's time to go," I said softly.

She sniffled slightly and nodded her head.

I turned around at the sound of the door opening. It was Roy.

"I forgot my bag," he said as he reached under one of the benches and pulled it out.

He looked over at us. "Are you still crying?"

Kia just sniffled in response. I knew she

wasn't any more happy about crying than she was about missing the shot.

Roy slowly shook his head. "You're not the only one who's upset you know."

"She feels bad enough as it is, Roy," I said.

"She feels bad? All of us are upset, even those of us who didn't miss the shot, but you don't see any of us crying, do you? This is why I didn't want you two on the team in the first place."

"Come on, Roy, give her a break!" I snapped.

"Don't give me a hard time," Roy said. "Remember what Mr. Roberts said ... we aren't teammates any more."

What a jerk! He was blaming Kia and already going back to threatening me and —

"Now all we are is friends," Roy said.

"Friends?" I echoed.

"Yeah. How many times to we have to go over this before you get it?"

"I think I understand," I said, holding my hands up in front of me.

"Good. Both of you go and see your parents. They're standing out there looking all nervous."

We both got up and grabbed our bags.

"And Kia," Roy said, "if anybody even

thinks about giving you a hard time about missing that shot, then you talk to me ... and I'll make sure nobody bothers you again. See you tomorrow."

Roy left, the door swinging shut behind him. Roy was one of the biggest surprises of my whole life. But that didn't help Kia right now.

"Are you okay?" I asked.

"Not right now, but I will be," she answered. "It'll take about a year."

"A year?" I asked.

She nodded her head and smiled. "Yeah. Until next year when we beat Vista Heights in the finals."

"Kia ...," I said, shaking my head slowly.

"What? Don't you think we can beat them next year?" she demanded. "We'll be a year older and bigger and better and —"

"That isn't it," I said, cutting her off. "I just don't know if Vista will make it to the finals next year. We might have to beat somebody else for the championship."

Kia flashed a big smile, and suddenly it wasn't just her who felt better.

**The adventures of Nick and Kia
continue in *Hoop Crazy*
coming in 2001!**

Other novels by Eric Walters:

*Rebound* (Stoddart, 2000)
*Caged Eagles* (Orca, 2000)
*The Bully Boys* (Penguin, 2000)
*The Money Pit Mystery* (HarperCollins, 2000)
*Three on Three* (Orca, 1999)
*Visions* (HarperCollins, 1999)
*Tiger by the Tail* (Beach Holme, 1999)
*The Hydrofoil Mystery* (Penguin, 1999)
*War of the Eagles* (Orca, 1998)
*Stranded* (HarperCollins, 1998)
*Diamonds in the Rough* (Stoddart, 1998)
*Trapped in Ice* (Penguin, 1997)
*STARS* (Stoddart, 1996)
*Stand Your Ground* (Stoddart, 1994)